簡愛

Jane Eyre

原著 _ Charlotte Brontë

改寫 _ Frances Mariani

譯者 _ 安卡斯

ABOUT THIS BOOK

For the Student

🎧 Listen to the story and do some activities on your Audio CD.

💬 Talk about the story.

⭐ Prepare for Cambridge English: Preliminary (PET) for schools

For the Teacher

 A state-of-the-art interactive learning environment with 1000s of free online self-correcting activities for your chosen readers.

Go to our Readers Resource site for information on using readers and downloadable Resource Sheets, photocopiable Worksheets, and Tapescripts. www.helblingreaders.com

For lots of great ideas on using Graded Readers consult Reading Matters, the Teacher's Guide to using Helbling Readers.

Level 4 Structures

Sequencing of future tenses	*Could* / *was able to* / *managed to*
Present perfect plus *yet, already, just*	*Had to* / *didn't have to*
First conditional	*Shall* / *could* for offers
Present and past passive	*May* / *can* / *could* for permission *Might* for future possibility
How long?	*Make* and *let*
Very / *really* / *quite*	Causative *have* *Want* / *ask* / *tell* someone to do something

Structures from lower levels are also included.

CONTENTS

ABOUT THE AUTHOR

Charlotte Brontë was born in 1816. Her father was a clergyman[1] and the family lived in a parsonage[2] in Haworth, a small village in Yorkshire. Her mother died when she was five and Charlotte and her brother and sisters were brought up[3] by their aunt. For a short time she attended a school with her older sisters Maria and Elizabeth and her younger sister, Emily. However, when Maria and Elizabeth both died of tuberculosis[4] in 1825, Charlotte and Emily left the school and their father taught them, and their brother Branwell, at home.

Charlotte worked for a short time as a governess[5] in England, and then went to Brussels to learn French and later to teach there.

On Charlotte's return to Yorkshire, she tried to open a school in Haworth together with her sisters Emily and Anne. But it was not a success because Haworth was too isolated. Instead she and her sisters turned to[6] writing.

In 1846 Charlotte persuaded her sisters to publish *Poems by Currer, Ellis and Acton Bell* (the sisters all had pseudonyms[7] because it was not common for women of the time to be writers). This was a commercial disaster. But in 1847 Charlotte's *Jane Eyre* was published and the book was an immediate success.

In 1854 Charlotte Brontë married Reverend A.B. Nicholls but she died the following year, aged only 39.

1 clergyman [ˈklɜˈdʒɪmən] (n.) 神職人員；牧師
2 parsonage [ˈpɑrsṇɪdʒ] (n.) 牧師公館
3 bring up 養育長大
4 tuberculosis [tjuˌbɜˈkjəˈlosɪs] (n.) 結核病
5 governess [ˈgʌvənɪs] (n.) 家庭女教師
6 turn to 開始
7 pseudonym [ˈsudṇˌɪm] (n.) 筆名

ABOUT THE BOOK

Jane Eyre (1847) is set[1] in the Yorkshire Dales[2] in Victorian Britain[3]. It was not a conventional[4] novel of the time, but was an immediate success with the reading public and is still popular today.

Jane Eyre is a story about growth[5], courage and love. The novel tells the story of a poor orphan[6] girl who grows up in a difficult environment. Jane Eyre's character evolves gradually. The reader can see Jane Eyre's passions as a young girl slowly turn to reason as she becomes a more mature and independent woman. For this reason the novel can be seen as a *Bildungsroman*[7].

---

1 set [sɛt] (v.) 為（小説、舞臺等）設置背景
  （動詞三態：set; set; set）
2 dale [del] (n.) 山谷
3 Victorian Britain 維多利亞時代的英國
4 conventional [kən`vɛnʃənl] (a.) 習慣的；傳統式的
5 growth [groθ] (n.) 身心的成長
6 orphan [`ɔrfən] (n.) 孤兒
7 Bildungsroman [`bɪlduŋsro,mɑn] (n.) 教育小説
8 boarding school 寄宿學校
9 presence [`prɛzn̩s] (n.) 容貌；出現；存在

The book is written as a first-person narrative by the protagonist Jane Eyre. In this way the reader has direct contact with Jane and her feelings and actions. Jane Eyre is a courageous woman who works hard to change and improve her situation.

After leaving her unloving aunt at Gateshead Hall, Jane Eyre goes to boarding school[8] at Lowood Institution. She learns to become a governess and gets her first job at Thornfield Hall. Jane soon falls in love with her employer, Mr Rochester. Their love is complicated because of her position as his governess but also for another important reason: the mysterious presence[9] in the attic of Thornfield Hall.

Jane Eyre does not stop loving Mr Rochester but she also wants to be a respected and independent woman. Her choices throughout the novel show her to be a strong and modern heroine of her time and one of the first feminist role models in literature. The novel deals with many themes including women's role in society, family, social class and forgiveness.

1 Look at these pictures of Jane Eyre. Match the correct description to each picture.

ⓐ Jane with her cousin in her aunt's home.

ⓑ Jane with her friend at boarding school.

ⓒ Jane with her pupil when she is a governess.

ⓓ Jane with her beloved as an independent woman.

2 What kind of person do you think Jane Eyre is? Work with a partner and write a list of possible words to describe her.

3 Jane Eyre is an orphan. Here is a definition of the word "orphan."

> **orphan** ['ɔrfən]
> (noun) a child whose parents are dead.

Look at these groups of different people in the story. Use a dictionary to help you with any words you do not understand. Match the correct title to the group of people.

❶ School   ❷ House   ❸ Family

_____ [a] aunt   uncle   cousin

_____ [b] teacher   superintendent   owner   monitor   pupil

_____ [c] governess housekeeper   servant   ward   maid

4 Match the titles from Exercise **3** to the sentences below.

_____ [a] Jane Eyre works as a governess at Thornfield Hall. Her little ward is called Adela. The housekeeper, Mrs Fairfax, is friendly and kind. Jane meets and gradually falls in love with the owner of the house, Mr Rochester.

_____ [b] The only nice teacher at Lowood is the superintendent Miss Temple. The owner, Mr Brocklehurst, is very strict.

_____ [c] When Jane Eyre's parents die she is sent to live with her aunt and uncle and her cousins: the Reed family.

5 Match the words from the story with the pictures.

slates
advertisement
stool
easel
piano
drawing
sewing
benches

a _____

b _____

c _____

d _____

e _____

THE SUN

**GOVERNESS
AVAILABLE**

f _____

g _____

h _____

6 Use each of the words from Exercise **5** to complete the following sentences.

a In the library there was an _____ for painting.

b I wanted to look for a new job so I decided to put an _____ in the newspaper.

c I was standing on a _____ in the middle of the room and everyone was looking at me.

d When Mr Brocklehurst entered the schoolroom, everyone stopped writing on their _____ and stood up.

e I decided to spend the afternoon doing some _____ for Adela's lessons the next day, so I went upstairs to get some paper and pencils.

f Grace Poole does the _____ and other jobs.

g Girls of all ages were sitting on wooden _____ on each side of long tables.

h I heard her invite him to sing while she played the _____.

7 Look at this picture of different kinds of rural Victorian transport. Match these words to the numbers in the picture.

on foot
open carriage
coach
on horse

8 Read the following text about Victorian Britain.

Queen
Victoria

The Victorian age in British history is named after Queen Victoria, who was Britain's queen from 1837 until 1901. Life in Victorian times was not the same as it is now. There were big differences in homes, schools, jobs and entertainments. No TV, no computers, and no central heating. Transport was very different too. Most people travelled on foot or by coach for longer distances. Only richer people had horses to ride or carriages to go out in. Train travel in the 1840s was still very rare because there weren't many railway lines. There were no cars (until the last few years of Victoria's reign). There was no air travel but only very long journeys on ships.

Work with a partner and write a list of the differences between life now and in Victorian times. Discuss with another pair.

1. Gateshead Hall

It was raining heavily and very cold outside. My aunt, Mrs Reed, was lying on a sofa in front of the fire in the drawing room[1]. Her three children Eliza, John, and Georgiana were sitting around her but she didn't want me there.

"Jane, you can sit with us when you become more pleasant," she said. "Now go away and be quiet."

I went into the breakfast room and chose a book from the bookcase[2]. Then I climbed into the window seat[3] behind the curtain with it.

Suddenly the door opened.

"Hello!" cried John Reed. Then he paused. He thought the room was empty.

"Where is she?" he continued. "Lizzy! Georgy! Jane isn't here. Tell mama she's gone out in the rain!"

Eliza put her head round the door. "She's behind the curtain, John."

I came out immediately. I didn't want to be pulled out by John.

"What do you want?" I asked.

1 drawing room 客廳
2 bookcase [ˋbʊk,kes] (n.) 書櫃
3 window seat（窗檻下的）窗座；窗檯

"Say, 'What do you want, Master Reed?'" John answered. He sat down in an armchair and continued, "I want you to come here."

John Reed was fourteen—four years older than me and he bullied[1] me continually. I was very afraid of him. No one in the house took my side[2]. The servants[3] were too afraid and his mother, Mrs Reed, didn't notice. I was completely alone.

I came up to his chair and he stuck out his tongue at me.

I knew that he wanted to hit me. As I looked at him I thought, "How ugly you are."

Maybe he knew what I was thinking because he suddenly lifted his hand and hit me hard. I fell back a step or two from his chair.

"That is for being rude to my mama," said John, "and for hiding behind curtains, and for looking at me in that way—you rat!"

I was sure he wanted to hit me again.

"What were you doing behind the curtain?" he demanded[4].

"I was reading."

1 bully [ˋbʊlɪ] (v.) 霸凌；欺侮
2 take my side 站在我這邊
3 servant [ˋsɝvənt] (n.) 僕人
4 demand [dɪˋmænd] (v.) 查問

"Show me the book."

I returned to the window seat and picked up the book.

"You have no right[5] to take our books. You aren't part of our family. You have no money. Your father left you nothing. You have no right to live here with gentlemen's children like us and eat the same meals that we eat and wear clothes that our mama buys for you. I'll teach you to take my books! Because they are mine. Everything in this house will be mine in a few years. Go and stand by the door."

I did and John threw the book at me. I fell and hit my head. It started to bleed[6] and was very painful. Suddenly I felt angry.

"Wicked[7] and cruel boy!" I said. "You are like a murderer! You are like the Roman emperors!"

"What! What!" he cried. "Did you hear her, Eliza and Georgiana? I'll tell mama!"

He ran towards me, grabbed[8] my hair and shook me. I fought back furiously[9].

"Rat! Rat!" he shouted.

Eliza and Georgiana ran to find Mrs Reed. They came back with Bessie the nurse[10] and Miss Abbot the maid[11] behind them.

"Can you believe it? She attacked Master John!" I heard someone say.

---

5 have no right 沒有權利
6 bleed [blid] (v.) 流血（動詞三態：bleed; bled; bled）
7 wicked [ˈwɪkɪd] (a.) 壞的；缺德的
8 grab [græb] (v.) 攫取；抓取
9 furiously [ˈfjʊərɪəslɪ] (adv.) 憤怒地
10 nurse [nɜ˞s] (n.) 奶媽；保姆
11 maid [med] (n.) 侍女；女僕

"Take her away to the red room," said Mrs Reed. "And lock the door."

Bessie and Miss Abbot took hold of me. I fought them and tried to escape[1].

"Hold her arms, Miss Abbot," shouted Bessie. "She's like a mad cat."

When we got to the red room, they pushed me onto a chair.

"Sit still or I'll tie your hands," said Bessie.

"I won't move," I promised and held the chair with my hands.

They stood and looked at me. Their faces were very serious.

"Don't forget, Miss," Bessie began, "that you owe[2] a lot to Mrs Reed. The only reason that you aren't in the poorhouse[3] is because she looks after[4] you."

I didn't reply. The words weren't new to me.

JANE

- What do we know about Jane? Tick (✓) the correct boxes.
  ☐ She is an orphan.
  ☐ She has no money.
  ☐ She is not happy.
  ☐ She is not welcome in the home where she lives.
  ☐ She has a good relationship with her cousins.
  ☐ She is a servant in the house.

---

1 escape [əˋskep] (v.) 逃跑；逃脫
2 owe [o] (v.) 欠；歸功於
3 poorhouse [ˋpʊrˏhaʊs] (n.) 救濟院；貧民所
4 look after 照顧

Then Bessie and Miss Abbot left me. They shut the door and locked it behind them.

The room was cold because it was never used. Mr Reed, my uncle, died in this room nine years ago and everyone believed the room was haunted by his ghost[1]. I couldn't remember my uncle but I knew that he was my mother's brother. My parents died when I was a baby and Mr Reed took me into his house. Before dying he made Mrs Reed promise to look after me and treat[2] me as one of her own children. Perhaps Mrs Reed tried but she was unable to[3] love me. I wasn't her child and I wasn't pretty or happy. How could I be happy?

I stayed in the red room all night. It was terrible. My mind was full of nightmares[4] and voices. I was so frightened[5] that I fainted[6].

When they found me in the morning, they called Mr Lloyd the doctor to look at me. He asked me lots of questions. He was a kind man and I told him about my cruel cousin, John Reed, and about my unhappiness.

Mr Lloyd listened to my story. Then he asked if he could talk to Mrs Reed. He suggested a solution[7] to everyone's problems. Mrs Reed must send Jane Eyre away to school.

Soon I was well again but nobody in the house talked to me and I was treated worse[8] than before. But things were changing.

1 be haunted by a ghost 鬧鬼
2 treat [trit] (v.) 對待
3 be unable to 無法
4 nightmare [ˈnaɪtˌmɛr] (n.) 夢魘
5 frightened [ˈfraɪtn̩d] (a.) 害怕的
6 faint [fent] (v.) 昏厥
7 solution [səˈluʃən] (n.) 解決辦法
8 worse [wɜs] (adv.) 較差地
9 festive [ˈfɛstɪv] (a.) 節慶的
10 cheer [tʃɪr] (n.) 歡呼；高興
11 exclude [ɪkˈsklud] (v.) 把……排除在外
12 nursery [ˈnɜsərɪ] (n.) 育兒室
13 for company 作伴

November, December, and half of January passed. Christmas and the New Year were celebrated at Gateshead Hall with the usual festive⁹ cheer¹⁰. Everyone exchanged presents and there were lots of dinners and evening parties. I was excluded¹¹ from all enjoyment of course.

In the evenings I sat on the stairs and watched while my cousins had fun. Then I went back to the lonely, silent nursery¹². I sat looking at the fire with only my doll for company¹³. Human beings must love something and I loved my doll.

LOVE

- Jane says: "Human beings must love something." Do you agree?
- Who and what do you love?

Only Bessie was nice to me and I preferred her to anyone else at Gateshead Hall. It was Bessie who, on the fifteenth of January, came running upstairs to find me in the nursery.

"They want to see you in the breakfast room," she told me in a great hurry. She pushed me to the top of the stairs and went back into the nursery.

I slowly went down the stairs and entered the room. My aunt was sitting by the fire. A tall man in black stood beside her.

"This is the little girl that I wrote to you about," said Mrs Reed.

The man turned his head towards me and looked at me for a long time.

"Your name, little girl?" he asked.

"Jane Eyre, sir," I replied.

"Well, Jane Eyre, and are you a good child?"

Mrs Reed answered for me, "The less said about that the better[1], Mr Brocklehurst."

"Oh dear," was his reply. "I don't like naughty children. Do you know where wicked people go after they die?"

"They go to hell," I answered.

"Do you say your prayers[2] night and morning?" continued Mr Brocklehurst.

"Yes, sir."

"Do you read your Bible?"

"Sometimes."

"And the Psalms[3]? I hope you like them?"

"No, sir."

"No? How shocking[4]! That proves you have a wicked heart. You must pray and ask God to change it."

"Mr Brocklehurst," interrupted Mrs Reed. "I hope you can accept this girl at Lowood School. She is deceitful[5] and a liar[6] and she must learn to be humble[7]. I would like to send her immediately. She will stay full-time and spend all the holidays there too."

"Of course, madam," said Mr Brocklehurst. "Your decisions are wise. We will teach Miss Eyre humility[8] and obedience[9]. Our girls are all humble and obedient. We have great success at Lowood School."

1　the less . . ., the better . . .
　　愈少……愈好
2　prayers [prɛrz] (n.)（複）祈禱文
3　Psalm [sɑm] (n.)（大寫）〈詩篇〉
　　（聖經的一卷）
4　shocking [ˈʃɑkɪŋ] (a.) 令人震驚的

5　deceitful [dɪˈsɪtfəl] (a.) 騙人的
6　liar [ˈlaɪɚ] (n.) 說謊的人
7　humble [ˈhʌmbl̩] (a.) 謙恭的；卑微的
8　humility [hjuˈmɪlətɪ] (n.) 謙卑；謙遜
9　obedience [əˈbidjəns] (n.) 服從

Mr Brocklehurst left and I was alone with Mrs Reed. She started sewing[1]. Neither of us said anything. I was feeling angry with her. She said I was deceitful and a liar but I wasn't. I tried hard to be good but nothing I did was good enough for my aunt. She wanted me to suffer[2].

After a while she looked up from her sewing.

"Go back to the nursery," she said.

I got up and went to the door, stopped and came back again. I had to tell her. I took a deep breath.

"I am not deceitful," I said. "And I'm not a liar. I don't say I love you, because I don't. I hate you more than anyone in the world, except[3] John Reed. Your daughter Georgiana tells lies, but I don't."

Mrs Reed looked at me.

"I will never call you aunt again," I continued. "I will tell people how you have treated me, how cruel you have been to me."

"How dare you[4] say that, Jane Eyre!"

"How dare I, Mrs Reed? How dare I? Because it is the truth. You think I have no feelings and that I can survive[5] without love or kindness. But I can't, and you have no pity[6]. You locked me in the red room because your wicked boy hit me. I'll tell anybody who asks me. I'll tell them the truth. People think you a good woman but you are bad and mean. You are deceitful!"

1 sew [so] (v.) 做針線活（動詞三態：sew; sewed; sewed/sewn）
2 suffer [ˈsʌfɚ] (v.) 遭受；受苦
3 except somebody 除了某人
4 how dare you 你竟敢
5 survive [səˈvaɪv] (v.) 活下來；倖存
6 have no pity 沒有憐憫心

2. Lowood School

A few days later Bessie woke me early. I had to leave Gateshead Hall that morning. Only Bessie accompanied[7] me to the coach[8]. Mrs Reed didn't want to see me.

"Goodbye!" I cried as we passed through the hall and went out the front door. I was happy to leave. I wanted to start my new life.

Bessie hugged and kissed me.

"Take care of her," she said to the guard as he helped me get into the coach.

It was fifty miles to Lowood. The coach journey[9] was long and I eventually[10] fell asleep[11].

I woke up when the coach stopped. It was now evening. A person like a servant was standing by the door of the coach.

"Is there a little girl called Jane Eyre here?" she asked.

"Yes," I answered.

The guard[12] lifted[13] me up and put me down on the ground next to my trunk[14]. Then the coach drove away.

---

7 accompany somebody 陪伴某人
8 coach [kotʃ] (n.) 馬車
9 journey [ˈdʒɜ˞nɪ] (n.) 行程
10 eventually [ɪˈvɛntʃʊəlɪ] (adv.) 最後地

11 fall asleep 睡著
12 guard [gɑrd] (n.) 護送者
13 lift [lɪft] (v.) 舉起
14 trunk [trʌŋk] (n.) 大行李箱

I looked around. Rain, wind and darkness filled the air. The servant girl and I went through a door of a big house. A tall, important-looking[1] lady met me in the hall. Behind her there was another lady.

Miss Miller then took me away. The house was very large and she led me through lots of different rooms. I could hear the hum[2] of voices in the distance. Finally, we entered a long room. Girls of all ages were sitting on wooden benches[3] on each side of long tables. The youngest were about nine or ten and the oldest were twenty. All of them were dressed in the same brown wool dresses and white pinafores[4]. They were studying their books. The hum of voices was the girls repeating their lessons over and over to themselves. The number of girls sitting at the tables seemed infinite[5]. I later learned there were eighty girls at Lowood School.

Miss Miller told me to sit on a bench near the door. She then walked to the top of the long room.

"Monitors[6]! Collect the books and put them away!" she cried out loudly.

Four tall girls collected the books from the girls at the tables.

"Monitors, fetch[7] the supper trays[8]!" Miss Miller cried out.

1　important-looking　(a.) 有地位的
2　hum [hʌm] (n.) 嗡嗡聲
3　bench [bɛntʃ] (n.) 長椅
4　pinafore [ˈpɪnə͵for] (n.) 圍兜
5　infinite [ˈɪnfənɪt] (a.) 無限的
6　monitor [ˈmɑnətɚ] (n.) 班長
7　fetch [fɛtʃ] (v.) 拿來；取物
8　tray [tre] (n.) 托盤

The tall girls handed out portions[1] of something from the trays. I couldn't eat because I was too excited and tired.

When the meal was over, Miss Miller read prayers. Then all the girls went upstairs to another very long room full of beds. Two girls got into each bed. That night I slept with Miss Miller. I fell asleep immediately. I was too tired even to dream.

SCHOOL

- What are Jane's first impressions of this school?
- How is this school different from your school? Discuss with a partner.

A loud bell rang the next morning to wake us up. It was still dark. It was very cold so I got dressed quickly. The bell rang again and we all went down to the schoolroom.

Miss Miller read prayers and then called out, "Form classes!"

For more than an hour we read the Bible in our different classes. After that we marched into another room for breakfast. I was very hungry but the smell of the food in front of us was terrible.

"Disgusting[2]! The porridge[3] is burnt again!" whispered[4] a girl.

"Silence!" shouted one of the teachers.

I quickly started eating but I stopped after one mouthful[5]. It really was too disgusting to eat. I looked around me. Spoons moved slowly.

I saw each girl taste the porridge and try to swallow[6] it but then most of them stopped eating too.

When the bell rang at the end of breakfast, everyone was still hungry.

I saw one of the teachers taste the porridge. "It's disgusting! How shameful[7]!" she whispered to another teacher.

We went back to the schoolroom and formed our classes again. Before starting our lessons, everybody stood up. The tall important-looking lady from the night before entered the room. I later learned her name was Miss Temple and she was the superintendent[8] of Lowood School. She taught the older girls.

When the clock struck twelve the superintendent stood up. "This morning you couldn't eat your breakfast," she said. "You must all be hungry. I have ordered a lunch of bread and cheese for you all."

The teachers looked at her in surprise.

"I'll take responsibility," she added and then she left the room.

We ate our bread and cheese happily and then went out into the garden.

1 portion [ˈporʃən] (n.) 一份
2 disgusting [dɪsˈɡʌstɪŋ] (a.) 令人作嘔的
3 porridge [ˈpɔrɪdʒ] (n.) 粥
4 whisper [ˈhwɪspɚ] (v.) 低聲說
5 mouthful [ˈmauθfəl] (n.) 一口；滿口

6 swallow [ˈswɑlo] (v.) 吞；嚥
7 shameful [ˈʃemfəl] (a.) 丟臉的；不體面的
8 superintendent [ˌsupərɪnˈtɛndənt] (n.) 監督人

The stronger girls ran around and played games but the pale, thin ones stood together trying to keep warm. Some of them had a bad cough[1].

I stood on my own and no one spoke to me. But I wasn't lonely or sad. Being alone was normal for me. I looked up at the school building and read the inscription[2] on a stone sign[3].

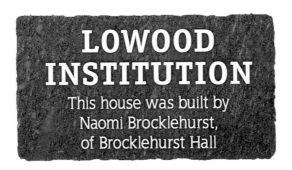

LOWOOD INSTITUTION
This house was built by
Naomi Brocklehurst,
of Brocklehurst Hall

I was thinking about the word "institution" when I heard someone coughing behind me. I turned and saw a girl sitting on a stone bench. She was reading a book.

"Is your book interesting?" I asked her.

"I like it," she answered, looking at me carefully.

"Can you tell me what the word 'institution[4]' means?" I asked.

"It means this school is partly a charity[5] school," she replied. "We are all charity children. I suppose you are an orphan like the rest of us?"

"Yes," I said.

"And who was Naomi Brocklehurst?" I asked, wanting to know more.

"The lady who built the new part of this house. She is dead and her son owns Lowood now."

"Then this house doesn't belong to that tall lady—the one who ordered the bread and cheese?"

"To Miss Temple? Oh, no, unfortunately! She works for Mr Brocklehurst."

MR BROCKLEHURST

- What do you remember about Mr Brocklehurst? Go back to page 22 and check.

"Does he live here?" I asked.

"No," she said. "He lives in a big house two miles away with his family. He is a clergyman⁶."

"Do you like the teachers here?"

"They're alright."

"How long have you been here?"

"Two years. But you ask too many questions," she said to me. "I want to read my book."

Just at that moment the dinner bell rang and we had to go in.

1 cough [kɔf] (n.) 咳嗽
2 inscription [ɪnˈskrɪpʃən] (n.) 銘文
3 sign [saɪn] (n.) 招牌；標牌

4 institution [ˌɪnstəˈtjuʃən] (n.) 機構
5 charity [ˈtʃærətɪ] (n.) 慈善
6 clergyman [ˈklɝdʒɪmən] (n.) 神職人員；牧師

3. Helen Burns

I soon learned the name of my new friend because one of the teachers continually criticized[1] her.

"Burns," she said (the teachers called us by our surnames). "Sit up straight!" Or: "Burns, don't look at me like that!"

One day, as a punishment[2], she had to stand in the middle of the schoolroom so that everybody could look at her.

When the girls in her class were tested, Burns knew all the answers. She knew more than all the other girls but the teacher never praised[3] her.

"Why are your nails so dirty, Burns?" was all she said to her.

I couldn't understand why the teacher punished her. She didn't do anything wrong. And every time she was punished or told off[4], she never got angry. The teacher often criticized her but she never reacted. She kept her usual calm, humble expression even when that teacher hit her with the stick[5]. I saw her cry only once.

In the evenings we were allowed to rest for a whole hour. One evening I found Burns sitting by the fire. She was reading the same book as before. I went and sat down next to her.

"What's your first name, Burns?" I asked her.

"Helen," she replied.

"Would you like to leave Lowood?"

"No! Why? I was sent here to get an education."

"But that teacher is so cruel to you!"

1 criticize [ˈkrɪtɪˌsaɪz] (v.) 批評
2 punishment [ˈpʌnɪʃmənt] (n.) 懲罰
3 praise [prez] (v.) 稱讚
4 tell off 責罵
5 stick [stɪk] (n.) 棍子

"Cruel? Not at all! She's strict[1]. I have faults[2] and she corrects them."

"But she hit you," I cried. "And you aren't a bad girl. You're very clever. How can you not be angry with her? If she hits me, I won't be able to keep quiet."

"You must," Helen replied. "Mr Brocklehurst expels[3] pupils[4] if they don't obey the rules. We must obey and not cause problems for other people. The Bible teaches us to love our enemies[5] and to be good to them even when they hurt us."

I couldn't believe it. How could Helen be so forgiving[6]? She didn't do anything wrong but the teacher hit her. She was a cruel, bad-tempered[7] woman.

"Does Miss Temple treat you badly too?" I asked.

"Oh, no," Helen replied. "Miss Temple is good. But when I make mistakes she tells me. It's bad to make mistakes and I must learn to be a better person. You're still young and you'll learn this."

"But Helen," I began. "If someone is unkind to me or punishes me unjustly[8], I dislike them. It's natural. Like it's natural to love someone when they are kind to you and accept punishment when you deserve[9] it."

I could see that Helen didn't agree with me. We didn't talk any more that evening.

POINTS OF VIEW

- Who do you agree with, Helen or Jane? Why? Discuss with a partner.

4. Mr Brocklehurst

My first winter at Lowood was long and hard. It often snowed and it was very cold. Our clothes didn't keep us warm. We were given very little food and were constantly[10] cold and hungry.

But the worst thing that happened to me that winter was Mr Brocklehurst's first visit to Lowood.

One afternoon soon after my arrival at Lowood, a tall black figure entered the schoolroom. I recognized Mr Brocklehurst immediately. Everybody stopped writing on their slates[11] and stood up. Even the teachers stood up. I felt very afraid. Mr Brocklehurst had false information about me from Mrs Reed. I was sure he wanted to tell everyone I was a liar.

He talked to Miss Temple about the school. He complained about a lot of things. The girls had too much to eat, their clothes were washed too often, some of the girls" hair wasn't completely straight and even that some of the girls were growing too tall. Miss Temple listened to these absurd[12] complaints and tried not to show her anger.

1 strict [strɪkt] (a.) 嚴格的

2 fault [fɔlt] (n.) 缺點；過失

3 expel [ɪk`spɛl] (v.) 開除

4 pupil [`pjupl] (n.) 小學生

5 enemy [`ɛnəmɪ] (n.) 敵人

6 forgiving [fɚ`gɪvɪŋ] (a.) 寬恕人的

7 bad-tempered [`bæd`tɛmpɚd] (a.) 脾氣不好的

8 unjustly [ʌn`dʒʌstlɪ] (adv.) 不公平地

9 deserve [dɪ`zɝv] (v.) 應受；該得

10 constantly [`kɑnstəntlɪ] (adv.) 不斷地

11 slate [slet] (n.) （書寫用的）石板

12 absurd [əb`sɝd] (a.) 荒謬的；可笑的

All this time I was hiding my face behind my slate because I didn't want Mr Brocklehurst to see me. But then to my horror[1] I dropped it. It fell to the floor and broke into pieces. Everybody turned to look at me.

"Ah, the new girl!" said Mr Brocklehurst. "I have something to say about her. Come here girl."

The girls next to me pushed me forward. Two monitors lifted me onto a stool[2]. The stool was in the middle of the room and everybody was looking at me.

"Girls! Teachers!" said Mr Brocklehurst. "Can you all see this girl? She is young and healthy. But I must warn you about her. She is evil and she is a liar! I learned this from her benefactor[3], Mrs Reed. That good lady treated her well but this girl was deceitful and dishonest. Mrs Reed sent this girl here to learn to be good and honest. Teachers! You must watch her and punish her when she is naughty. Girls! You must not play with her or speak to her. Perhaps we'll manage to[4] save her soul. Now she will stay on the stool for another half hour."

With these words Mr Brocklehurst left the room.

My punishment was so unjust. I felt furious[5] and humiliated[6]. My face was burning and it was difficult for me to breathe. I couldn't look at anyone.

1 horror [ˋhɔrɚ] (n.) 恐怖
2 stool [stul] (n.) 凳子
3 benefactor [ˋbɛnəˏfæktɚ] (n.) 捐助人
4 manage to 設法……
5 furious [ˋfjʊərɪəs] (a.) 狂怒的
6 humiliate [hjuˋmɪlɪˏet] (v.) 使丟臉

But then someone walked past me. It was Helen Burns. When she passed again she looked up at me and smiled. What a smile! I remember it now. Her smile gave me strength and I stood on my stool with my head up high.

HUMILIATION

- Why is Jane's punishment unjust?
- Have you ever felt humiliated?
  Discuss with a partner.

The clock struck[7] five. My half hour was over so I got off the stool and went to the corner of the now empty room. I started to cry. I was trying so hard to be good at Lowood and to make a new start. I was good at[8] my schoolwork[9] and the teachers liked me. But now everybody thought I was a liar. This made me cry even harder.

Then Helen arrived. She brought me some coffee and bread from the dining room but I didn't want to eat or drink anything. Helen sat down next to me while I continued to cry.

I spoke first. "Helen, why do you stay with me? Everybody thinks I am a liar and hates me."

---

7 strike [straɪk] (v.) 打；擊
   （動詞三態：strike; struck;
   struck/stricken）

8 be good at 擅長……
9 schoolwork [ˋskul͵wɝk]
   (n.) 課業

"They don't hate you. They pity you," Helen replied. "No one likes Mr Brocklehurst. They'll quickly forget his words if you continue to be a good girl. You'll see. Their coldness will soon change to kindness."

I didn't say anything. Helen made me feel calm[1]. I put my head on her shoulder and my arms around her. I was still holding her when a figure[2] approached[3] It was Miss Temple.

"I came to find you, Jane Eyre," she said. "I want to talk to you. Helen Burns, you can come too."

We followed her to her room and she told us to sit down.

"Have you finished crying?" Miss Temple asked me, looking at my face.

"No," I replied.

"Why not?"

"Because I have been wrongly accused[4]. And you, ma'am[5], and everybody else, will now think I'm wicked."

"Well, Jane," Miss Temple said kindly. "I'd like to hear what you have to say. Tell me your story, but I want the truth."

So I told Miss Temple my story. I tried to include[6] all the facts and the names of the people involved[7]. I also included my own faults and tried hard not to show my feelings of hate.

---

1 calm [kɑm] (a.) 平靜的
2 figure [ˈfɪgjɚ] (n.) 身影
3 approach [əˈprotʃ] (v.) 接近
4 accuse [əˈkjuz] (v.) 指控
5 ma'am [mæm] (n.) 女士
6 include [ɪnˈklud] (v.) 包括
7 involved [ɪnˈvɑlvd] (a.) 牽扯在內的

Miss Temple looked at me for a few minutes in silence. Then she said, "I know Mr Lloyd, the doctor you talked about. I will write to him. If he tells me the same things as you have told me, you will be publicly[1] cleared[2] of every accusation[3]. For me, Jane, you are clear now."

With these kind words Miss Temple kissed me and then turned to Helen.

"How is your cough tonight, Helen?"

"It is a little better," Helen replied.

Miss Temple then called for tea and toast. That evening we feasted[4] on food, warmth, kindness and affection[5].

About a week later, Miss Temple received an answer from Mr Lloyd. He said that I was telling the truth. That day Miss Temple announced[6] to everyone that Jane Eyre wasn't guilty[7] of Mr Brocklehurst's accusations. The teachers kissed me and my companions all smiled at me. I was so happy.

1 publicly [ˋpʌblɪklɪ] (adv.) 公開地
2 clear [klɪr] (v.) 為（某人）辯白
3 accusation [͵ækjəˋzeʃən] (n.) 指控；指責
4 feast [fist] (v.) 盛宴款待
5 affection [əˋfɛkʃən] (n.) 溫情
6 announce [əˋnauns] (v.) 宣布
7 guilty [ˋgɪltɪ] (a.) 有罪的
8 typhus [ˋtaɪfəs] (n.) 斑疹傷寒
9 fever [ˋfivɚ] (n.) 發燒
10 transform [trænsˋfɔrm] (v.) 使改變；改造
11 woods [wʊdz] (n.) 森林；樹林
12 occasion [əˋkeʒən] (n.) 場合；時刻
13 determine [dɪˋtɝmɪn] (v.) 決定；決心

5. Illness

My name now cleared, I worked very hard at my lessons. I was moved to a higher class and I started to learn French and drawing.

Spring came and brought warmer weather but it also brought typhus[8]. Many girls caught the fever[9] and in May part of Lowood was transformed[10] into a hospital.

Little food and bad coughs and colds made pupils weak. Forty-five of the eighty girls at the school were ill. Classes were less frequent and rules were relaxed because the teachers were all busy with the patients. Some girls were sent home either to escape the fever or to die. Some died at the school.

Lowood became an even sadder place and was filled with fear. The only way to escape was to go out into the garden. There we could enjoy the warm spring weather, the flowers and walks in the woods[11].

I remained healthy but my dear friend Helen Burns didn't. She was taken to a room upstairs and I wasn't allowed to see her. I often thought about her and asked the teachers how she was. On one occasion[12] I was given the answer, "She won't be with us for much longer."

I knew this meant death and not a journey back to her home. I was determined[13] to see her once more before she died.

A nurse told me that she was in Miss Temple's room so I went to find her.

She was lying in bed behind a curtain.

"Helen," I whispered softly. "Are you awake?"

"Is that you, Jane?" she asked in her sweet voice.

I got on her bed and kissed her. Her body was thin and cold.

"I've come to see you, Helen."

"You came to say goodbye. I think you are just in time."

"Where are you going, Helen? Are you going home?"

"Yes. To my last home."

"No, no, Helen!" I cried.

"Stay with me, Jane. Don't leave me!" Helen said. "I am very happy. I am going to God. He loves me. Hold me, Jane."

"Good night, Helen. I won't leave you. I'll stay with you."

She kissed me and I kissed her and we both fell asleep.

That night Helen died in my arms.

Many girls died of the fever—so many that people began to ask questions. They soon learned about the awful[1] conditions[2] in the school and changes had to be made. Mr Brocklehurst no longer had so much control. A committee[3] made the decisions. These changes were all good for us pupils. There was more comfort, more compassion[4], and, more importantly, more food. The school started slowly to become a really useful institution.

---

1 awful [ˈɔful] (a.) 可怕的
2 conditions [kənˈdɪʃənz] (n.) （複）條件
3 committee [kəˈmɪtɪ] (n.) 委員會
4 compassion [kəmˈpæʃən] (n.) 慈悲

I spent another eight years at Lowood: six as a pupil and two as a teacher. I studied and worked hard and learned a lot in this time. Then Miss Temple, who was a mother, teacher and later a companion to me, married and left the school. I missed her a lot and I began to think it was time for me to leave Lowood too.

I thought long and hard about what to do. In the end I decided to put an advertisement[1] in the newspaper.

A young lady is looking for a job as a governess[2] in a private[3] family with children under fourteen years of age. She is qualified[4] to teach all general subjects[5] including French, drawing and music.

A few days later I received a reply.

A private family requires a governess for a little girl under ten years of age. The salary[6] is thirty pounds[7] a year. Please send references[8] and details to Mrs Fairfax, Thornfield, near Millcote.

---

1 advertisement [ˌædvəˈtaɪzmənt] (n.) 廣告;宣傳
2 governess [ˈgʌvənɪs] (n.) 家庭女教師
3 private [ˈpraɪvɪt] (a.) 私人的
4 qualified [ˈkwɑləˌfaɪd] (a.) 合格的
5 general subject 通識科目
6 salary [ˈsælərɪ] (n.) 薪水
7 pound [paʊnd] (n.) 英鎊
8 reference [ˈrɛfərəns] (n.) 推薦函

I read the letter carefully. I hoped so much that the job and the family were respectable[1]. I was alone in the world and had no one to give me advice[2].

I told the superintendent about the job, adding that the salary was good. I also asked her to tell Mr Brocklehurst and the committee. I wanted to ask them for references.

Mr Brocklehurst said that I had to ask Mrs Reed for permission[3] because she was my legal[4] guardian[5]. So I wrote to her. I received a letter back saying, "I could do what I wanted". The committee eventually gave me permission to leave and the necessary references.

Now I was all ready to become a governess at Thornfield Hall!

CHANGE

- Discuss with a partner. Why do you think Jane wants to leave Lowood School?
- How do you think she feels?
- Do you think Jane is ambitious?
- Are you ambitious?

1 respectable [rɪˈspɛktəbl̩] (a.) 體面的
2 advice [ədˈvaɪs] (n.) 忠告
3 permission [pəˈmɪʃən] (n.) 允許
4 legal [ˈligl̩] (a.) 法定的
5 guardian [ˈgɑrdɪən] (n.) 保護者

6. Thornfield Hall

It took sixteen hours to get to Millcote so I had lots of time to think about my new employer Mrs Fairfax. I hoped she wasn't another Mrs Reed. When I arrived, a carriage[6] was waiting to take me to Thornfield Hall.

Two hours later it stopped in front of a large, long house. A girl opened the door and I went inside.

She took me to a small comfortable room with a cheerful[7] fire. A little old lady was sitting next to it. She was knitting[8].

"How do you do, my dear?" she said, getting up to meet me. "You've had a long journey. Come to the fire. You must be cold."

"Mrs Fairfax?" I asked.

"Yes. Please sit down."

She helped me take off[9] my bonnet[10] and shawl[11] and told the girl to take them to my room.

"Then bring Miss Eyre something to eat," she said.

"She's treating me like a visitor," I thought. I wasn't expecting such kindness from an employer[12].

---

6 carriage [ˈkærɪdʒ] (n.) 馬車
7 cheerful [ˈtʃɪrfəl] (a.) 使人愉快的；
   興高采烈的
8 knit [nɪt] (v.) 編織（動詞三態：
   knit; knit/knitted; knit/knitted）
9 take off 脫下

10 bonnet [ˈbɑnɪt] (n.) 有帶子的女帽
11 shawl [ʃɔl] (n.)
   方形披巾

12 employer [ɪmˈplɔɪɚ] (n.) 雇主

"Will I have the pleasure of seeing Miss Fairfax tonight?" I asked.

"Miss Fairfax? Oh, you mean Miss Varens! Adela Varens is the name of your pupil."

"Oh! Then she isn't your daughter?"

"No, I have no family. I'm glad that you've come. Thornfield can be lonely in the winter. Before I only had the servants to talk to. But now Adela, her nurse and you are here, so we'll all have a happy time together."

Mrs Fairfax continued to talk while I ate. I liked her more and more.

That night I slept very well. Mrs Fairfax was kind and my room was safe and warm.

When I woke up the next morning it was already light. The room looked lovely in the sunlight. It was very different from the one I had at Lowood.

"I'm going to like working here," I thought happily.

I got dressed and went to explore[1]. Downstairs the front door was open so I went out into the garden. It was a lovely autumn day and I could see trees and hills in the distance[2]. As I was enjoying the view and the fresh air, Mrs Fairfax appeared at the door.

"How do you like Thornfield?" she asked.

I told her I liked it very much.

"Yes," she said, "it's a pretty place. But Mr Rochester needs to spend more time here."

"Mr Rochester!" I exclaimed[3]. "Who's he?"

"The owner[4] of Thornfield," she replied. "Didn't you know?"

"I thought that Thornfield belonged to[5] you."

"To me? My dear child! What an idea! I'm only the housekeeper[6]."

MR ROCHESTER

- What do you think Mr Rochester will be like?
- Make a list of what we know about him so far.
- Add to your list as you continue reading.

"And the little girl—my pupil?"

"She's Mr Rochester's ward[7]. He asked me to find a governess for her. Look! Here she is with her nurse."

A pretty little girl with long curly[8] hair ran towards us.

"Good morning, Miss Adela," said Mrs Fairfax. "Say hello to Miss Eyre. She's going to teach you and make you a clever lady."

"Bonjour[9]," said Adela. She turned to her nurse, who was standing behind her, and asked her a question in French.

"Does she speak English?" I asked Mrs Fairfax.

---

1 explore [ɪk'splor] (v.) 探索
2 in the distance 遠處
3 exclaim [ɪks'klem] (v.) 叫喊著說出
4 owner ['onɚ] (n.) 擁有人
5 belong to somebody 屬於某人
6 housekeeper ['haʊsˌkipɚ] (n.) 女管家
7 ward [wɔrd] (n.) 受監護的未成年人
8 curly ['kɝlɪ] (a.) 鬈髮的
9 bonjour〔法〕早安

"A little, but Sophie, her nurse, doesn't speak any at all," said Mrs Fairfax.

I was glad my French[1] was good and Adela was very happy to discover I spoke her language.

"You speak French as well as Mr Rochester does," she exclaimed.

She told me that after her mother died, Mr Rochester brought her and Sophie from France to England in a great ship. Then they came to live at Thornfield. Now Mr Rochester was no longer here and he never came to see her.

After breakfast, Adela and I went to the library. This was our schoolroom. There were books, a globe[2], a piano and an easel[3] for painting.

We had lessons until noon, then I sent Adela back to Sophie. I decided to spend the afternoon doing some drawings for Adela's lessons the next day so I went upstairs to get some paper and pencils.

When I was on the stairs, Mrs Fairfax called to me from a room that she was cleaning.

"Your morning school hours are over now, I suppose."

I went back down to speak to her. The room was very grand[4]. It had purple chairs and curtains and there was a Turkish carpet on the floor.

1 French [frɛntʃ] (n.) 法文
2 globe [ɡlob] (n.) 地球儀
3 easel [ˋizl̩] (n.) 畫架
4 grand [ɡrænd] (a.) 華麗的；雄偉的

"What a beautiful room!" I exclaimed as I looked round. "And how tidy[1] you keep it."

"Yes," Mrs Fairfax replied. "Mr Rochester's visits here are rare[2]. But they are always sudden and unexpected. He often brings visitors. I like to have everything ready for him when he comes."

"What's Mr Rochester like?" I asked.

"He's a gentleman, a good master and respected by everyone. He's very clever but perhaps he's a little strange."

"In what way, strange?"

"I don't know. It isn't easy to describe[3]. It's difficult to understand if he's happy or not."

Then Mrs Fairfax showed me all the other rooms in the house—downstairs and upstairs. Finally, she took me out through the attic[4] and onto the roof.

"The view is wonderful from here," she said.

The garden and the countryside looked lovely in the bright autumn light and when we came in again, the attic seemed very, very dark. Suddenly I heard a strange noise. It was a low laugh. I stopped and listened. Then I heard it again.

"Did you hear that laugh?" I asked Mrs Fairfax. "Who was it?"

"One of the servants, I expect," she answered. "Perhaps it was Grace Poole."

---

1 tidy ['taɪdɪ] (a.) 整潔的
2 rare [rɛr] (a.) 稀有的
3 describe [dɪ'skraɪb] (v.) 描述
4 attic ['ætɪk] (n.) 閣樓；頂樓房間

I heard the noise again.

"Grace!" exclaimed Mrs Fairfax.

The door of one of the attic rooms opened and a woman came out. She was about forty years old and she had red hair and a plain[1] face.

"There's too much noise, Grace," said Mrs Fairfax. "Remember your orders[2]!"

The woman nodded[3] silently and went in.

"Grace works here. She does the sewing and other jobs," Mrs Fairfax told me. "Now, tell me, how was your pupil, Miss Adela, this morning?"

Grace Poole was immediately forgotten and our conversation about Adela continued until we got downstairs.

GUESS

- Why does Grace Poole have to work in the attic?
- What are the orders that she must remember?

---

1 plain [plen] (a.) 相貌平常的
2 order ['ɔrdə] (n.) (v.) 命令
3 nod [nɑd] (v.) 點頭
4 sensible ['sɛnsəbl] (a.) 明理的
5 affectionate [ə'fɛkʃənɪt] (a.) 充滿深情的
6 spoiled [spɔɪlt] (a.) 被寵壞的
7 progress ['prɑgrɛs] (n.) 進步
8 relief [rɪ'lif] (n.) 慰藉
9 corridor ['kɔrɪdə] (n.) 走廊
10 offer ['ɔfə] (v.) 提供
11 halfway ['hæf'we] (adv.) 在中途
12 gallop ['gæləp] (n.) (馬)疾馳
13 crash [kræʃ] (n.) 撞擊聲

7. Mr Rochester

I was happy at Thornfield Hall. Mrs Fairfax was a kind, calm, sensible[4] person. My pupil was a lively, affectionate[5] child and tried hard to please me. She was difficult to teach at first because she was spoiled[6] but she soon became obedient and made good progress[7] in her lessons.

I had no reason to complain about my life at Thornfield Hall but I was often bored. My only relief[8] was to walk—sometimes around the garden, sometimes up and down the corridor[9] on the third floor, and other times on the roof.

When I was on the third floor, I often heard Grace Poole laughing. There were days when she was very quiet but there were other days when she laughed loudly. Sometimes when I saw her, I spoke to her but she never wanted to talk and went back to her room in the attic.

October, November and December passed. In January, Adela caught a cold and wasn't well enough to do her lessons. Having the afternoon free, I offered[10] to walk to Hay, a village two miles away, to post a letter for Mrs Fairfax. It was a very cold day so I walked fast to keep warm.

I was nearly halfway[11] there when the sound of a horse galloping[12] at great speed broke the silence. I stopped and waited for it to pass.

A moment later I heard a loud crash[13]. I ran back to see what it was.

（34）The horse and its rider were on the ground.

"Are you injured[1], sir?" I asked.

The man didn't reply so I asked again, "Can I do anything?"

"Please, just move out of my way[2]," he answered.

He was a man of about thirty-five with black hair and a dark complexion[3]—not very handsome. I didn't feel afraid or shy. In fact his angry expression[4] made me like him so I didn't move away.

"I cannot think of leaving you, sir," I said. "It's late and you are alone. I must be sure that you are able to ride your horse before I go."

He looked at me when I said this. It was the first time his eyes met mine.

"Why aren't you at home?" the man asked me. "Where have you come from?"

"From Thornfield," I answered. "I'm going to Hay to post a letter."

"Whose house is Thornfield?"

"Mr Rochester's."

"Do you know Mr Rochester?"

"No, I've never seen him."

"You aren't a servant at the hall, of course. You are . . ." He stopped. He looked at my clothes. He seemed puzzled[5] about what I was so I helped him.

1 injured [ˈɪndʒəd] (a.) 受傷的
2 move out of my way 讓開
3 complexion [kəmˈplɛkʃən] (n.) 膚色
4 expression [ɪkˈsprɛʃən] (n.) 表情
5 puzzled [ˈpʌzld] (a.) 困惑的

"I'm the governess."

"Ah, the governess!" he repeated. "Of course. The governess!"

He tried to stand up but the pain in his leg was very bad.

"I don't want you to go and get help," he said. "But you can help me a little yourself, if you will be so kind."

"Yes, sir."

"Try to bring my horse to me."

I tried to catch the horse but it was very excited and I wasn't able to take hold of it. The man waited and watched for some time and then he laughed.

"I see," he said. "If my horse won't come to me, I must go to my horse. Please come and help me."

He put his hand on my shoulder and we slowly walked to his horse. He caught it easily and jumped on it despite[1] the pain in his ankle[2]. He was obviously[3] a good horseman[4].

THE HORSEMAN

- Who do you think this man is?

"Thank you," he said. "Now go quickly to Hay and post your letter. Then hurry home as fast as you can."

He rode away with his dog running after him.

I posted my letter in Hay and walked back to Thornfield. It was getting dark now. I stopped for a few minutes at the place where I met and helped the traveler.

The incident[5] was unimportant but it gave me something to think about. A new face, a new memory[6]. I didn't want to go back to Thornfield straight away. I didn't want to lose that memory and return to my safe but boring life there.

It was completely dark when I eventually opened the door of Thornfield Hall and went in. I could hear voices in the dining room. One of them was Adela's. I went to Mrs Fairfax's room. A dog, just like the traveler's dog, was sitting in front of the fire.

I called a servant to ask for information. "Whose dog is this?"

"He came with the master, Mr Rochester. He has just arrived and is with the others in the dining room. John has gone to get the doctor because the master had an accident. His horse fell and he hurt his ankle."

"I see," I said.

I took a candle and I went upstairs to change my dress before dinner.

---

1 despite [dɪ'spaɪt] (prep.) 儘管
2 ankle ['æŋkl] (n.) 腳踝
3 obviously ['ɑbvɪəslɪ] (adv.) 顯然地
4 horseman ['hɔrsmən] (n.) 騎馬者
5 incident ['ɪnsədn̩t] (n.) 事件
6 memory ['mɛmərɪ] (n.) 記憶

I didn't see Mr Rochester again that night. He followed the doctor's orders and went to bed early.

The next day there was a lot of movement[1] and life in the house.

Adela was very excited too. "Mr Rochester has a present for me," she told me. "It's in his trunk."

Late in the afternoon when the house was quieter, Mrs Fairfax came to my room.

"Mr Rochester would like you and Adela to have tea with him in the drawing room later," she said. "You must change your dress. I'll help you."

"Is it really necessary?" I asked.

"Yes," she replied "When Mr Rochester is at Thornfield, I always do."

Adela was already sitting at Mr Rochester's feet by the fire. He didn't look up to greet us as we entered the room so we sat down quietly and waited. Mrs Fairfax tried to make conversation but Mr Rochester neither spoke nor moved. When the tea tray was brought in, Adela and I moved to the table but he stayed on his sofa.

"Please take Mr Rochester his tea," Mrs Fairfax said, giving me his cup.

"Did you bring Miss Eyre a present too?" asked Adela as Mr Rochester took the teacup from my hand.

"A present?" said Mr Rochester, turning to look at me for the first time. "Did you expect a present, Miss Eyre?"

"No, sir," I replied. "You don't know me and I've done nothing to deserve one."

"That isn't true," Mr Rochester replied. "You have done good work with Adela. She has made a lot of progress."

"Sir," I said. "That is my present. Praise of her pupils' progress is the best thing you can give a teacher."

"Humph!" said Mr Rochester and he drank his tea in silence.

"Come nearer the fire!" he said when tea was over.

He began asking me questions about Lowood and my family situation². Then he ordered me to play a tune on the piano and show him some of my drawings. He was obviously trying to test me. He wanted to provoke³ me and see how I reacted.

---

1 movement [ˈmuvmənt] (n.) 搬動
2 situation [ˌsɪtʃuˈeʃən] (n.) 情況；處境
2 provoke [prəˈvok] (v.) 挑釁；激怒

39

But I was strong and able to play his game. So, I replied to his questions politely[1] using the same tone of voice as he used with me.

At last, tired of our company, he told us all to go to bed.

PROVOCATION

- Are you easily provoked?
- How do you react when people provoke you?

"I think Mr Rochester is strange and complicated[2]," I said later to Mrs Fairfax.

"Maybe," she replied. "But we must forgive him for that. It's partly his nature but also because he has many problems."

"What kind of problems?" I asked.

"Family problems. Many are linked[3] to this house. I think that's why he never stays at Thornfield for long periods of time."

I wanted to know more but it was clear from Mrs Fairfax's expression that she didn't want to talk any more about him.

---

1 politely [pə`laɪtlɪ] (adv.) 禮貌地
2 complicated [`kɑmplə͵ketɪd] (a.) 複雜的；難懂的
3 link [lɪŋk] (v.) 聯繫

8. The Fire

For the next few days I saw little of Mr Rochester. He was always busy or out on his horse.

One evening, however, he sent for Adela and I after dinner. He was in a good mood[4] and gave Adela the present she was waiting for.

"Now go away and open it," he said. "And don't bother me any more with your chatter[5]."

Then he turned to me and said, "Come and sit over here, Miss Eyre. I want to be able to see you without having to change my position[6] in this comfortable chair."

He sat looking into the fire for a couple of minutes and I observed[7] him for the same amount of time. He had large dark eyes. They were fine eyes, full of great feeling.

"You're examining me, Miss Eyre," he said, looking at me. "Do you think I'm handsome?"

"No, sir," I replied without thinking.

"Ha, ha," he laughed. "You're a very unusual girl, Miss Eyre. You look very serious and quiet but when you have to answer questions you're surprisingly frank[8] and honest."

---

4 in a good mood 好心情
5 chatter ['tʃætɚ] (n.) 喋喋不休
6 position [pə'zɪʃən] (n.) 位置；姿勢

7 observe [əb'zɝv] (v.) 看到；觀察
8 frank [fræŋk] (a.) 坦白的

I was embarrassed[1] and tried to apologize[2]. But he liked my honesty. That evening we talked for a long time. I learned that he didn't have a very good opinion[3] of himself because of a mistake he made in his past. He regretted[4] it now and wanted to be a better person. He also wanted to find happiness.

One afternoon, a short time after our long talk, I was outside with Adela when Mr Rochester suddenly appeared. Adela starting playing with his dog so Mr Rochester and I walked around the garden. He talked about his past and about Adela.

"She was the daughter of a Parisian[5] dancer named Celine Varens," he said. "I was once in love with Celine but she deceived me and ran away to Italy with another admirer[6]. She left her daughter, Adela, in Paris. She said I was the child's father but I know I'm not. I don't know who is. The poor little girl has no one else and I want to help her. I don't know why I'm telling you all this. I hope you won't leave now you know the story. Are you shocked[7]?"

"No," I replied. "I will love Adela even more now I know."

And so Mr Rochester and I gradually[8] became friends. He was less moody[9] and often wanted to talk. Our conversations made me happy and filled a gap[10] in my life.

I felt alive[11] when I was with him. He was trying to be a better person but there was always the presence[12] of an unknown[13] sadness inside him that was still a mystery[14] to me.

1 embarrassed [ɪmˋbærəst] (a.) 尷尬的
2 apologize [əˋpɑləˌdʒaɪz] (v.) 道歉
3 opinion [əˋpɪnjən] (n.) 意見
4 regret [rɪˋgrɛt] (v.) 後悔
5 Parisian [pəˋrɪzɪən] (a.) 巴黎的
6 admirer [ədˋmaɪrɚ] (n.) 仰慕者
7 shocked [ʃɑkt] (a.) 感到震驚的
8 gradually [ˋgrædʒʊəlɪ] (adv.) 漸漸地
9 moody [ˋmudɪ] (a.) 鬱鬱寡歡的
10 gap [gæp] (n.) 缺口
11 alive [əˋlaɪv] (a.) 有活力的
12 presence [ˋprɛzn̩s] (n.) 容貌；出現；存在
13 unknown [ʌnˋnon] (a.) 未知的
14 mystery [ˋmɪstərɪ] (n.) 難以理解的事物

SADNESS

- What kind of events in life make people very sad?
- What could be the cause of the unknown sadness that Mr Rochester has inside him?

That night I lay in bed and thought about Mr Rochester. "Will he leave Thornfield soon?" I wondered. "Mrs Fairfax says he never stays here very long. He's been here for eight weeks now. The house will be a sad place if he goes."

Then suddenly I heard a strange sound. It seemed to be above me. I sat up; my heart was beating[1] fast. A clock struck two. Someone or something passed the door of my room.

"Who's there?" I called.

There was no answer. I began to feel frightened. Then I heard the low deep laugh. Was it Grace Poole? I had to find out[2]. I got up and went out into the corridor. I was surprised to see a candle burning there. And then I noticed[3] smoke and the smell of burning.

The smoke was coming from Mr Rochester's bedroom. The door was open so I went inside. The curtains around his bed were on fire[4]!

1 beat [bit] (v.) 擊；打（動詞三態：beat; beat; beat/beaten）
2 find out 查明
3 notice [`notɪs] (v.) 注意
4 on fire 著火
5 washbasin [`waʃ,besn] (n.) 臉盆
6 jug [dʒʌg] (n.) 罐；壺
7 throw [θro] (v.) 丟；拋（動詞三態：throw; threw; thrown）
8 flame [flem] (n.) 火焰
9 flood [flʌd] (n.) 水災
10 lying [`laɪɪŋ] (a.) 橫臥的（lie 的現在分詞）
11 depressed [dɪ`prɛst] (a.) 感到沮喪的

"Wake up! Wake up!" I shouted, but he didn't move.

I ran to the washbasin[5], picked up the water jug[6] and threw[7] the water on the flames[8]. Then I threw the water from a vase onto Mr Rochester's face and finally he woke up.

"Is there a flood[9]?" he cried finding himself lying[10] in a pool of water.

"No, sir," I answered. "But there was a fire."

"What happened?" he asked, getting out of his wet bed.

He listened with a very serious look on his face while I told him.

Then he said, "I must go to the attic. Stay here until I return. Don't move or call anyone."

When he came back, he looked pale and depressed[11].

"It's just as I thought," he said.

"What is, sir?" I asked.

"You said that you heard a laugh. Have you heard that laugh before?"

"Yes, sir. The woman who sews—Grace Poole. She laughs like that. She's a strange person."

"Exactly[1]. Grace Poole—you are right. She is, as you say, strange—very. Jane, only you and I know about this incident. Do you understand me? Please say nothing to the servants. I'll talk to them about it tomorrow. Now we must sleep."

"Yes, sir. Good night, then, sir," I said, turning to leave.

"Where are you going, Jane?" Rochester exclaimed.

"You told me to go, sir."

"But you must say goodbye properly[2]. You have just saved[3] my life! At least shake hands with me."

He held out his hand. I gave him mine. He took it and held it in both his hands, looking at me with a strange fire in his eyes.

"I knew you were a special person as soon as I saw you. You're good for me, Jane."

"I'm glad I was awake," I said and went back to my room but I couldn't sleep.

---

1 exactly [ɪɡˋzæktlɪ] (adv.)（用於回答）一點也不錯
2 properly [ˋprɑpəlɪ] (adv.) 恰當地
3 save [sev] (v.) 救

9. Blanche Ingram

I both wanted and was afraid to see Mr Rochester after my sleepless night. But I didn't meet him the following day[1]. When I went past his room later I found Grace Poole sewing new curtains for his bed. I couldn't believe it and I felt I had to test her.

"Good morning, Grace," I said. "What a strange incident! Did Mr Rochester really not wake anybody up? And didn't anyone hear him putting out[2] the fire?"

She raised[3] her eyes to me and said, "Perhaps you heard a noise, Miss?"

"I did," I said quietly. "I heard a strange laugh."

She looked at me again and said, "Then I think you should lock your door carefully every night."

At that moment a servant entered the room. She told me that Mrs Fairfax was waiting for me so I had to leave Grace Poole.

For the rest of the day I thought about this mystery. Why didn't Mr Rochester punish Grace Poole for what she did? I wanted to see him to ask him. I asked Mrs Fairfax where he was.

"Mr Rochester has gone to visit friends on the other side of Millcote," she told me. "They're having a big party."

"Will he come back tonight?" I asked.

"Oh, no. I think he'll stay there for a week or more. He's popular at their parties, especially with the ladies."

"Which ladies?" I asked.

"Most of them," she replied. "But in particular with Blanche Ingram. She's the most beautiful of all. I saw her when she came here for a Christmas ball⁴."

"What's she like?"

JANE

- Why is Jane surprised at Mr Rochester?
- Why does she ask about Blanche Ingram?
- What do you think Jane feels for Mr Rochester?

"Tall with a good figure, lovely olive⁵ skin and eyes like jewels⁶. And she has wonderful hair! Dark with the glossiest⁷ curls you ever saw. She can sing well, too. I even heard her sing with Mr Rochester."

Alone in my room that night I forced⁸ myself to look in the mirror.

---

1 the following day 隔天
2 put out 熄滅
3 raise [rez] (v.) 抬起
4 ball [bɔl] (n.) 舞會

5 olive [ˋɑlɪv] (a.) 橄欖色的
6 jewel [ˋdʒuəl] (n.) 寶石
7 glossy [ˋglɔsɪ] (a.) 有光澤的
8 force [fors] (v.) 逼迫

"Fool!" I told myself, looking at my reflection[1]. "You are a poor governess with a plain face. How can you think you are important to Mr Rochester? Think of Blanche Ingram and remember who you are."

Two weeks went by and there was no news of Mr Rochester. I tried to forget my feelings for him. I worked hard with Adela and in my free time I sewed and drew. I wanted to be busy. I even thought about leaving Thornfield and getting another job.

Then a letter arrived. I waited anxiously[2] while Mrs Fairfax read it.

"Does Mr Rochester say when he's coming home?" I asked, trying not to sound interested.

"Yes, he does," she replied. "He's arriving with a big party of[3] guests in three days. We have to get the house ready for their arrival."

There was lots to do. Even Adela and I were asked to help in the preparations[4].

One afternoon while we were working, I heard two of the servants talking about Grace Poole.

"At least she is well paid," said one.

"Oh yes," the other replied. "She gets five times[5] our salary. But she deserves it for the job she has to do."

Then they noticed I was listening and quickly walked away.

So now I knew for sure that there was a mystery at Thornfield but I still didn't really know any more about it.

---

1 reflection [rɪˋflɛkʃən] (n.) 倒影；鏡影
2 anxiously [ˋæŋkʃəslɪ] (adv.) 心急地
3 a party of 一夥……人
4 preparations [ˌprɛpəˋreʃənz] (n.)（複）準備工作
5 time [taɪm] (n.) 倍

SALARIES

- Why do you think Grace Poole has such a good salary?
- Do you think people should have different salaries for different jobs?
- What kind of people have the highest/lowest salaries in your country? Discuss with a partner.

The guests arrived—some in carriages, others on horseback. Adela and I watched them from an upstairs window. A beautiful lady was riding next to Mr Rochester. She matched[1] Mrs Fairfax's description[2] of Blanche Ingram.

The following evening Adela and I were called down to join[3] the party. Adela was soon making friends with all the ladies while I sat alone in a corner observing the scene. Blanche Ingram was without doubt the most beautiful woman in the room, even if her expression was a little haughty[4].

After coffee, she and Mr Rochester stood near the fireplace talking. I heard her invite him to sing while she played the piano. I listened to them for a while and then left through a side door.

I was on the stairs when Mr Rochester called me back.

"How are you, Jane?" he asked.

"I am very well, sir."

---

1 match [mætʃ] (v.) 相配
2 description [dɪˋskrɪpʃən] (n.) 描繪

3 join [dʒɔɪn] (v.) 加入
4 haughty [ˋhɔtɪ] (a.) 傲慢的

"Why didn't you come and speak to me in the drawing room?"

"I didn't want to disturb you. You seemed busy, sir."

"You look pale and a little depressed," he said. "What's wrong? Tell me."

"Nothing—nothing, sir. I'm not depressed."

"Well, tonight I excuse you. But while my visitors are here, I'd like you to come and join our party every evening. I insist. Now, good night, my . . ."

He stopped, bit his lip, turned round and walked away.

In the days that followed I watched Mr Rochester and Blanche Ingram. Although I loved Mr Rochester I wasn't jealous of Miss Ingram. She had no qualities[1] to be jealous[2] of. She was pretty and could play the piano and sing nicely but her mind was empty. Her conversation was learned from books, nothing she said was original[3]. She wasn't tender[4] or sympathetic[5] and she had no interest in Adela. It was clear, however, that Mr Rochester intended to marry her, perhaps for family reasons, perhaps political[6] reasons, or perhaps because her position in society[7] and connections[8] were useful to him. But I knew that he didn't love her.

---

1 quality [ˈkwɑlətɪ] (n.) 特質
2 jealous [ˈdʒɛləs] (a.) 妒忌的；吃醋的
3 original [əˈrɪdʒənl̩] (a.) 原創的
4 tender [ˈtɛndɚ] (a.) 溫柔的
5 sympathetic [ˌsɪmpəˈθɛtɪk] (a.) 同情的

6 political [pəˈlɪtɪkl̩] (a.) 政治的
7 society [səˈsaɪətɪ] (n.) 社會
8 connections [kəˈnɛkʃənz] (n.) （複）人脈

10. Secrets

One night, while the guests were still at Thornfield, a man arrived and asked to speak to Mr Rochester.

"My name is Mason and I've just arrived from the West Indies[9]," he said.

He asked me to inform Mr Rochester of his arrival so I went to look for him and found him in the library.

"His name is Mason, sir, and he comes from the West Indies. From Spanish Town[10], in Jamaica[11], I think."

On hearing the name Mr Rochester suddenly turned very pale. He grabbed my hand and seemed to stop breathing.

"Mason! The West Indies!" he said in a strange voice.

"Do you feel ill, sir?" I asked.

"I feel weak, Jane," he said almost falling.

"Oh! Lean[12] on me, sir."

"Jane, you offered me your shoulder once before. I'll have it again now."

"Yes, sir. Here! Take my arm."

He sat down and made me sit beside him. Holding my hand in both of his, he looked at me with worried eyes.

"My little friend!" he said. "I'd like to be on a desert[13] island with only you. I'd have no problems then."

---

9 West Indies 西印度群島
10 Spanish Town 西班牙鎮 (位於牙買加)
11 Jamaica [dʒə'mekə] (n.) 牙買加

12 lean [lin] (v.) 倚；靠 (動詞三態：
　 lean; leaned/leant; leaned/leant)
13 desert [ˈdɛzət] (n.) 沙漠

"Can I help you, sir? I'd do anything for you."

"Bring him to me, Jane, and then leave us."

"Yes, sir."

I did this and much later, when I was in bed, I heard Mr Rochester show Mr Mason to his room. I hoped that was the end of Mr Rochester's troubles.

In the middle of the night I was woken by a terrible scream[1]. Then I heard a man calling for help[2]. A little later Mr Rochester knocked on my door.

"Are you up and dressed, Jane?"

"Yes, sir."

"Then come with me. Be as quiet as you can."

I followed him up to the attic. I expected to see Grace Poole there and was surprised to see Mr Mason. He was alone. He was sitting on a chair and one of his arms was covered in blood.

"Clean his wound[3]," Mr Rochester said to me. "I'm going to get the doctor. Don't speak to this man while I'm away—not a word! And Richard, if you open your mouth and frighten this girl, you'll know all the force[4] of my anger!"

He left and locked the door. I was scared but I followed his instructions[5] and cleaned Mr Mason's wound in silence[6].

"What is this mystery?" I thought. "First fire and now blood."

I was glad when Mr Rochester came back with the doctor. He put a bandage[7] on the wound and then helped Mr Rochester take Mr Mason down the stairs. They put him into a carriage and he left just before the servants woke up.

---

1 scream [skrim] (n.) 尖叫聲
2 call for help 呼喊求救
3 wound [waund] (n.) 傷口
4 force [fɔrs] (n.) 力量
5 instructions [ɪnˈstrʌkʃənz] (n.) （複）指示
6 in silence 在沉默中

It was getting light now and the spring air was fresh and clean. Mr Rochester suddenly picked a rose from a bush[8] and gave it to me.

"Thank you again, Jane," he said taking my hand and holding it tightly.

The following afternoon I received a message[9] from Gateshead Hall. John Reed was dead and my aunt, Mrs Reed, was dying. She wanted to see me.

I went immediately to ask Mr Rochester for permission[10] to leave. I found him playing billiards[11] with Miss Ingram.

When he saw me, he followed me out of the room.

"Well, Jane?" he said.

"Sir, please can I go away for a week or two?"

"To do what? To go where?"

I explained about my aunt. Mr Rochester didn't understand why I wanted to go but finally he gave me some of my wages[12] and made me promise to return.

"I'd like to say something else, sir," I said. "I believe you are planning to marry Miss Ingram. When you do, Adela should go to school. You won't need me any more so I'll look for a new job."

7 bandage [ˈbændɪdʒ] (n.) 繃帶
8 bush [buʃ] (n.) 灌木叢
9 message [ˈmɛsɪdʒ] (n.) 消息
10 permission [pəˈmɪʃən] (n.) 允許；許可
11 billiard [ˈbɪljəd] (n.) 撞球
12 wage [wedʒ] (n.) 薪水

I didn't want to be at Thornfield with Blanche Ingram as Mrs Rochester.

"Don't do that yet, Jane," he said.

And again he made me promise to return as soon as possible before eventually letting me go.

When I arrived at Gateshead Hall, Bessie met me and gave me tea. Everything in the house was the same and memories of my life there started to come back to me[1].

Later, Bessie took me to see Mrs Reed in her bedroom. I was determined to forget my feelings of bitterness[2] and hate towards this woman. I wanted very much to forgive all her wrongdoings[3].

I went up to her. Her face was still stern[4] and hard. She didn't respond[5] when I touched or kissed her. I knew then that her feelings for me were the same as when I was a child. I was a bad girl in her mind and she had no intention[6] of changing her opinion of me. This hurt me and then it made me angry, but I was determined not to let her upset[7] me.

My aunt wanted to tell me something but she waited until she was sure we were alone.

"Well, Jane Eyre," she said. "I have done two bad things to you. I regret them now and I don't want to die without telling you about them. The first thing—I promised my husband to bring you up as my own child and I broke that promise. The other—well, go to my jewelry box, open it, and take out the letter you'll see there."

I did as she instructed and brought her the letter.
"Read it," she said.

> Madam,
>
> Will you please send me the address of my niece, Jane
> Eyre, and tell me how she is? I would like to write and
> ask her to come and live with me in Madeira⁸. I have a
> good job but I have never married and have no children.
> I'd like to adopt⁹ her and then leave her everything I
> have when I die.
>
> JOHN EYRE, Madeira.

The date on the letter was three years before.
"Why didn't you tell me about this?" I asked.
"Because I disliked you too much and didn't want to help you
in any way. I've never forgotten how you spoke to me when you
were a child."

---

1 come back to me 想起;記起
2 bitterness ['bɪtənɪs] (n.) 痛苦
3 wrongdoing ['rɔŋ'duɪŋ] (n.) 壞事
4 stern [stɜn] (a.) 嚴厲的
5 respond [rɪ'spɑnd] (v.) 回應
6 intention [ɪn'tɛnʃən] (n.) 意向
7 upset [ʌp'sɛt] (v.) 使心煩(動詞
　三態:upset; upset; upset)
8 Madeira [mə'dɪrə] (n.) 馬得拉
　(大西洋的群島)
9 adopt [ə'dɑpt] (v.) 收養

MRS REED

- How did Jane Eyre speak to her aunt when she was a child? Go back to page 24 if you don't remember.
- Do you remember bad things people did to you or can you forgive and forget? Discuss with a partner.

"I'm sorry, Aunt. I was only a child," I said.

She wasn't interested in my apology[1] and continued talking. "I took my revenge[2] on you. I wrote to your uncle and told him you were dead. There! I have said it. Now do what you want. You were born to[3] be my torment[4]."

"Don't think about it again, Aunt," I replied. "Kiss me and let us forget the past."

I put my lips near her cheek but she moved her head away. She couldn't love me even now.

"Love me or hate me, then, as you like," I said at last. "I forgive you everything. Ask God to do the same and be at peace[5]."

That night Mrs Reed died.

My plans were to stay at Gateshead only for a week or two but it was a month before I started my journey back to Thornfield.

---

1 apology [əˈpɑlədʒɪ] (n.) 道歉
2 revenge [rɪˈvɛndʒ] (n.) 報復
3 be born to 天生就……
4 torment [ˈtɔrmɛnt] (n.) 痛苦或苦惱的根源
5 at peace 處於平靜的狀態
6 tremble [ˈtrɛmbl̩] (v.) 顫抖

11. Back to Thornfield

I decided to walk to Thornfield Hall from Millcote because I didn't want Mrs Fairfax to send a carriage for me. It wasn't a particularly nice summer evening when I set out but I saw many farmers working in the fields.

I felt glad but I wasn't sure why. It wasn't my home that I was going to and I had no real friends there. "But Mrs Fairfax and Adela will be happy to see you," I told myself. "However, you know very well that you're thinking of someone else, and that he isn't thinking of you."

I was anxious to get to the house as soon as I could so I took the shorter way across the fields. Suddenly there he was! Mr Rochester himself, sitting on a wall with a book and pencil in his hands.

"Jane Eyre," he said. "Where have you been? Have you forgotten me?"

"Of course not, sir," I replied. Why was my body trembling[6]? Why was it so difficult for me to speak?

"Well, hurry home and rest your tired feet," he said, getting off the wall to let me pass.

I wanted to walk away calmly but something made me stop and turn round. "Thank you, Mr Rochester," I said. "I am strangely glad to get back again to you. Where you are is my home, my only home."

Then I walked away so fast that Mr Rochester had no possibility of catching up with[1] me.

Everyone at Thornfield Hall was glad to see me and I felt loved. After tea Mrs Fairfax, Adela and I sat together in Mrs Fairfax's room, happy to be in each other's company again.

The weather was beautiful that summer—the sun shone every day. One evening, after putting Adela to bed, I went out into the garden to enjoy the cool air. I soon discovered that I wasn't the only person taking an evening walk.

"Thornfield is a pleasant place in summer, isn't it, Jane?" Mr Rochester said.

"Yes, sir."

"You must be fond of[2] the house now. It's a shame[3] that you must move on[4]."

"Must I move on, sir?" I asked. "Must I leave Thornfield?"

"I really think you must, Jane, because I'm going to get married next month. I've found you a new job in Ireland."

The news came as a shock. I tried to stay calm but tears started to run silently down my face.

"Ireland is a long way away, sir," I said.

---

1 catch up with somebody 追趕上某人
2 be fond of 喜歡……
3 shame [ʃem] (n.) 憾事
4 move on 離開

"It is, Jane, and I'm very sorry I have to send you away. I sometimes have a strange feeling about you—especially when you are near me like now. I feel that there's a string[1] going from my heart to yours and that it is tied with a tight knot[2]. I feel that if I am separated[3] from you, the string will break and I will be hurt. But you don't feel like this. I think you will forget me."

"I'll never forget you, sir. But if I have to leave, I will. I love Thornfield. I've never been happier. The thought of never seeing you again fills me with great sadness. But if I have to leave . . ."

"Why do you have to leave?"

"Because of your bride[4], sir."

"My bride! What bride? I have no bride!"

"But you will have."

"Yes. I will!"

"Then I must go. You've told me yourself."

"No! You must stay," he said taking me in his arms. I tried to free myself of his embrace[5] but he held me tighter.

"Jane, please don't push me away! You're like a wild frantic[6] bird that is trying to escape."

"I'm not a bird and I have no cage or net around me. I am a free person. I can make my own decisions about my life. Now let me go!"

I pulled myself free and stood in front of him.

"Then decide your own destiny[7]," he said. "I offer you my hand, my heart, and a share of all my possessions[8]. Marry me, Jane!"

1 string [strɪŋ] (n.) 線
2 knot [nɑt] (n.) 結
3 separate [ˈsɛpəˌret] (v.) 分離

I didn't know what to reply. I thought he was making fun of[9] me.

"Can I believe you?" I said eventually. "Do you truly love me? Do you sincerely want me to be your wife?"

"I do. I do."

"Then, sir, I will marry you."

"Edward! Not 'sir,' my little wife!"

In the morning I wondered if Mr Rochester's proposal[10] was only a dream. To be sure that it wasn't, I needed to hear the words again so after breakfast I went to find him.

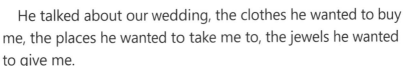

"My little Jane Eyre!" he said kissing me. "Soon to be Jane Rochester!"

At that moment I felt something stronger than joy—I think it was almost fear.

He talked about our wedding, the clothes he wanted to buy me, the places he wanted to take me to, the jewels he wanted to give me.

"I don't want jewels," I told him. "But there are two things I want to ask you. The first is: why did you pretend[11] that you wanted to marry Miss Ingram?"

4 bride [braɪd] (n.) 新娘子
5 embrace [ɪmˋbrɛs] (n.) 擁抱
6 frantic [ˋfræntɪk] (a.) 發狂似的
7 destiny [ˋdɛstənɪ] (n.) 命運
8 possessions [pəˋzɛʃənz] (n.)（複）財產
9 make fun of 嘲弄
10 proposal [prəˋpozl̩] (n.) 求婚
11 pretend [prɪˋtɛnd] (v.) 假裝

"Because I wanted to make you love me as much as I love you and I know jealousy helps love," he replied. "And the second thing?"

"Please talk to Mrs Fairfax about our marriage. She's a good person and I like her very much. I don't want her to have a bad opinion of me."

Mr Rochester promised and I went to my room. Later I went downstairs to see her.

She looked at me calmly and said, "I can't believe it. Are you really going to marry him? Does he love you?" she asked.

This hurt me and my eyes filled with tears.

"I'm sorry to upset you," Mrs Fairfax said. "But I must warn you to be careful. Things are not always what they seem to be."

A month passed and my wedding day approached. My trunk was packed[1] and my dress and veil were hanging[2] in the wardrobe[3].

Then one night while Mr Rochester was away on business[4], I woke up suddenly after a bad dream. A candle was burning in my room. I looked around and saw a tall female[5] figure near the wardrobe. She was looking at my wedding dress. She took out the veil, put it on and looked at herself in the mirror. Then she pulled it off and tore it into two pieces. I saw her face in the mirror. It was dark and savage[6]! I think I fainted from fear.

---

1 pack [pæk] (v.) 裝入行李
2 hang [hæŋ] (v.) 懸掛
　（動詞三態：hang; hung; hung）
3 wardrobe [ˈwɔrd.rob] (n.) 衣櫥

4 on business 為了生意
5 female [ˈfimel] (a.) 女性的
6 savage [ˈsævɪdʒ] (a.) 野蠻的

The night before our wedding I told Mr Rochester about the woman. It was Grace Poole, he said. I wanted to believe him but I wasn't convinced[1].

"I can see that you are nervous, Jane," he said. "Sleep with Adela tonight and lock the door from the inside."

I did and I felt safe with my arms around the little girl, but I couldn't sleep.

Early the next morning Sophie helped me put on my wedding dress. I didn't recognize[2] myself when I looked in the mirror before going downstairs.

Mr Rochester was impatient[3] to get to the church and made me walk so fast that I was out of breath when we reached the gate.

The church was very quiet. The only people there were the vicar[4] and his clerk[5] and two shadowy[6] figures in a corner looking at the Rochester tombs. Then the service began. The vicar announced our intention to get married and asked us if there was a reason why we shouldn't.

At that moment, a voice at the back of the church said, "The marriage cannot take place[7]."

"Continue!" shouted Mr Rochester angrily.

"I can't continue," said the vicar, "until we know what the problem is. Sir, tell us why the marriage cannot take place."

The speaker came forward. He introduced himself as Mr Briggs, a solicitor[8] from London.

"Because Mr Rochester is already married," he said. "And his wife is still living."

I looked at Mr Rochester. His face was deathly⁹ white.

"Have you got proof¹⁰?" demanded Mr Rochester.

Mr Briggs took a piece of paper out of his pocket and read it to us.

"I can prove¹¹ that on the 20th October (then a date fifteen years ago) Edward Rochester married my sister Bertha Antoinetta Mason in Spanish Town, Jamaica. I, myself, have a copy of the marriage certificate¹². Signed, Richard Mason."

Then he said there was a witness¹³ to prove that the lady was still living.

A pale face appeared behind Briggs. It was Mr Mason.

"Can you tell us if Mr Rochester's wife is still living?"

"She is. At Thornfield Hall," said Mason slowly. "I saw her there last April. I am her brother."

"At Thornfield Hall!" exclaimed the vicar. "Impossible! I've lived here for years, sir, and I've never heard of a Mrs Rochester at Thornfield Hall."

"That is because I made sure no one heard of it," said Mr Rochester. "Come with me, all of you. We'll go to Thornfield Hall and I'll show you my 'wife.'"

---

1 convinced [kən'vɪnst] (a.) 確信的
2 recognize ['rɛkəɡ,naɪz] (v.) 承認
3 impatient [ɪm'peʃənt] (a.) 急盼的
4 vicar ['vɪkɚ] (n.) 教區牧師
5 clerk [klɜk] (n.) 教堂執事
6 shadowy ['ʃædoɪ] (a.) 陰影的
7 take place 發生

8 solicitor [sə'lɪsətɚ] (n.) 律師
9 deathly ['dɛθlɪ] (a.) 像死的
10 proof [pruf] (n.) 證據
11 prove [pruv] (v.) 證明
12 certificate [sə'tɪfəkɪt] (n.) 證明書
13 witness ['wɪtnɪs] (n.) 證人

Mr Rochester took my hand and we hurried back to Thornfield. I was again without breath when we arrived, but this time it was because of the shock. The vicar, his clerk, Mr Briggs and Mr Mason followed us.

THE "WIFE"

- Have you guessed who Mr Rochester's wife is?
- How do you think Jane Eyre is feeling at this moment?

We all went upstairs to the attic. Grace Poole was sitting near the fire, but she wasn't alone. At one end of the room a figure was running up and down like an animal. It was growling[1] like a dog. When it saw Mr Rochester it stood up and moved the hair that fell over its face. I recognized it at once[2]. The woman who tore my veil!

Suddenly she threw herself at Mr Rochester and tried to bite him. She was strong but he managed to hold her arms. Grace Poole helped him tie her to a chair.

"That is my 'wife'!" he said. "Look at her! Then look at the young innocent[3] girl I wanted to marry. Can you blame[4] me for wanting a little happiness? Now go! I must make sure that my real wife is locked safely in."

---

1 growl [graʊl] (v.) 咆哮
2 at once 立刻
3 innocent [ˋɪnəsn̩t] (a.) 無罪的；清白的
4 blame [blem] (v.) 指責

12. Escape

I went to my room and took off my wedding dress. I sat down—tired and weak—and started thinking. Yesterday I was Jane Eyre, almost a bride. I had love and hope. Today I had nothing.

I still loved Mr Rochester but I knew I could not stay with him.

It was late afternoon when I finally got up and opened my door. Mr Rochester was sitting on a chair outside my room waiting for me.

"You've come out at last," he said. "Jane, will you ever forgive me?"

I forgave him immediately but I didn't tell him.

"Give me your hand, Jane. I want to explain everything. Just listen to me for a few minutes. Please!"

He told me that his father forced him to marry Bertha because her family was rich and his family needed money. He didn't know about her madness[1] until it was too late.

"We can go away," he continued. "Away from Thornfield and start a new life."

"No," I said. "I must leave you and Thornfield. I love you more than ever but I can't stay. I must begin a new life. Your wife is still living and I won't be your mistress[2]."

Mr Rochester begged[3] me to stay with him and I wanted to say yes but I couldn't.

I packed my few things in a parcel[4] and left Thornfield.

I knew that I had to get as far away as possible from there and the man I loved. Two days later the coach left me at a place called Whitcross.

I had no money now and I was completely alone. I started to walk. I walked for a very long time although I was tired and very hungry. Then it started to rain hard. I looked around for shelter[5] and finally found a small cottage[6]. Through the window I could see two girls with an old lady. I knocked on the door and asked for help but the old lady told me to go away. I was so exhausted[7] that I fell just outside the door, all my hope and strength gone.

"I'm going to die," I said aloud to myself.

"All men must die," said a voice in the darkness.

"Who's there?" I asked, terrified.

A man appeared and knocked loudly on the door.

"Is it you, Mr St John[8]?" asked the old lady inside.

"Yes, yes. Open quickly, Hannah." Then he said to me, "Stand up young woman and go in."

With difficulty I obeyed[9] him. Soon I was sitting in a clean, bright kitchen with a cup of hot milk and some bread in front of me. One of the girls asked my name.

"Jane Elliot," I replied.

"Are you lost? Can we get in touch with[10] your family or friends?" asked the man.

---

1 madness [ˈmædnɪs] (n.) 神經錯亂
2 mistress [ˈmɪstrɪs] (n.) 情婦
3 beg [bɛg] (v.) 懇求
4 parcel [ˈpɑrsl] (n.) 小包裹
5 shelter [ˈʃɛltɚ] (n.) 避難處
6 cottage [ˈkɑtɪdʒ] (n.) 農舍；小屋
7 exhausted [ɪgˈzɔstɪd] (a.) 精疲力竭的
8 St John 發音為 [ˈsɪndʒən]
9 obey [əˈbe] (v.) 遵守；聽從
10 get in touch with somebody 與某人聯繫

"I'm alone in the world," was my answer.

Later they took me upstairs and put me into a warm, dry bed.

For the next three days I slept. I had a fever and couldn't move.

On the fifth day I felt well enough to get up. I slowly and quietly went downstairs to the kitchen to meet the kind people who were looking after me. Hannah, the older lady and servant, was baking[1] bread. She smiled at me and told me to sit by the fire. She began to ask me questions.

"Have you been begging a long time?" she said.

I was shocked and told her that I wasn't a beggar.

"Why haven't you got a home or money, then?" she asked.

"I'll find a job and a home as soon as I can," I replied.

Then she told me the two girls, Diana and Mary Rivers, were sisters and the man, St John, was their brother. He was a vicar in the next village.

At that moment they all came in. They greeted me kindly and I thanked them for their hospitality[2]. They had lots of questions for me too. I explained my situation without giving them too many details[3].

"I'm not married and I have no home," I began. "I was at Lowood School and worked there as a teacher. Then I found a position as a governess. But, a few days ago I had to leave. I can't tell you why. I didn't do anything wrong—I'm not a criminal[4]. Now I must find work and earn my own money again."

---

1 bake [bek] (v.) 烘烤
2 hospitality [ˌhɑspɪˈtælətɪ] (n.) 殷勤招待
3 detail [ˈditel] (n.) 細節
4 criminal [ˈkrɪmənl] (n.) 罪犯

"So you're a teacher?" said St John. "A new church school for girls is opening here next month. I haven't found a teacher for it yet. The pay will be thirty pounds a year, and there's a cottage for the schoolmistress[1] to live in. Would you like to be this schoolmistress?"

"Thank you, Mr Rivers. Yes, I would, very much," I replied.

I spent a few more happy weeks with the Rivers and then we all went our different ways—I moved to my cottage, Diana and Mary back to their jobs as governesses and St John to his vicarage[2].

Miss Jane Elliot

My students at the school were simple village girls and farmers' daughters. I taught them to read, knit, sew and sing. I worked hard and was always busy but I was happy with my job. It was only at night that I remembered my past life. I often imagined[3] meeting Mr Rochester once again.

St John came every day to teach an hour of religion at the school, and during the holidays he came to visit me. On one particular visit he asked to look at my drawings.

I showed them to him with pleasure. He complimented[4] me on my skill[5] as he turned over the sheets[6] of paper. Then suddenly he stopped. He was looking at the blank[7] sheet I rested my hand on while painting. I don't know what he saw on it but he got up quickly, said goodbye and left.

1 schoolmistress [ˋskul‚mɪstrɪs] (n.) 女教員
2 vicarage [ˋvɪkərɪdʒ] (n.) 牧師住宅
3 imagine [ɪˋmædʒɪn] (v.) 想像
4 compliment [ˋkɑmpləmɛnt] (v.) 讚美
5 skill [skɪl] (n.) 技巧
6 sheet [ʃit] (n.) 一張（紙）
7 blank [blæŋk] (a.) 空白的

13. A New Life

The next day St John came back.

"I want to have a little talk with you," he said. "Come and sit with me near the fire."

When we were both seated[1], he took an envelope out of his pocket and held it up.

"A few weeks ago I received this letter from a Mr Briggs in London," he said. "It contains details of a girl called Jane Eyre. Yesterday I saw that name on a piece of paper among your drawings. You aren't Jane Elliot, are you? You are Jane Eyre."

"Mr Rivers, does the letter mention Mr Rochester?" was all I could think of to say.

"No," he replied. "Mr Briggs wants to find Jane Eyre because he has something important to tell her. He put an advertisement in the newspapers and a Mrs Fairfax saw it and wrote to him. She gave him the details. Mr Briggs wants to tell you that your uncle, Mr Eyre of Madeira, has died and left you all his money. You are a rich woman now."

"Me! Rich?"

"Yes. You have twenty thousand pounds."

I looked at him in astonishment[2].

"But, tell me," I said when I found my voice. "Why did Mr Briggs write to you about me?"

(69) "My mother's name was Eyre. She had two brothers—one who married Miss Jane Reed of Gateshead and John Eyre who went to Madeira. Mr Briggs was Mr Eyre's solicitor. He contacted[3] us when he couldn't find you."

"So your mother was my father's sister?"

"Yes."

"And therefore my aunt?"

He nodded.

"So you three, Diana, Mary and yourself, are my cousins?"

"Yes!"

I clapped my hands with joy! I had a family, people I could love and who were kind to me. I was no longer alone.

"I am so, so glad!"

"You are happier to hear you have cousins than to hear you have a fortune."

"Of course! Before I was alone and now I have a family. Write to Diana and Mary tomorrow and tell them to come home. With my money they will no longer have to work."

FAMILY

- With a friend draw Jane's family tree.
- Do you think having a family is important? Why?

1 seat [sit] (v.) 使就座
2 astonishment [əˈstɑnɪʃmənt] (n.) 驚訝
3 contact [kənˈtækt] (v.) 聯繫

I decided to share the twenty thousand pounds between the four of us. I gave up my teaching job at the school and moved back to the cottage to live with my cousins, Diana and Mary. St John still lived at the vicarage but he often visited us. This was a happy time for me.

One day St John told us that he was going to India to work as a missionary[1]. He started learning Hindustani[2] and asked me to help him. I agreed and after that we spent many hours studying together. As I got to know him better, I realized[3] that he was a very serious person. He was also very difficult to please.

I still thought about Mr Rochester a lot. I knew I couldn't visit him but I wanted to know how he was. I decided to write to Mrs Fairfax.

Two months passed without a reply. I wrote again. Day after day the post arrived but there was never anything for me. This upset me greatly.

Summer came and one sunny morning St John invited me to go for a walk. While we were resting on a rock, he asked me to marry him and go with him to India.

I said no straightaway[4], perhaps too quickly. I didn't love St John and I don't believe he really loved me. He just wanted me to help him with his missionary work.

I knew that my heart still belonged to Mr Rochester. I desperately[5] wanted news of him so I decided to go to Thornfield and find out for myself how he was.

---

1 missionary [ˈmɪʃənˌɛrɪ] (n.) 傳教士
2 Hindustani [ˌhɪnduˈstænɪ] (n.) 印度斯坦語
3 realize [ˈrɪəˌlaɪz] (v.) 認識到
4 straightaway [ˈstretəˌwe] (adv.) 立刻
5 desperately [ˈdɛspərɪtlɪ] (adv.) 絕望地

I told my cousins I was going away for a few days. They didn't ask me where.

I took a coach most of the way and then walked the last two miles to Thornfield. I walked quickly, sometimes even running. I was happy to see the woods again but most of all I couldn't wait to see Mr Rochester's face.

I finally arrived at the wall that surrounded[1] the garden. I turned the corner, anxious to see the house. I expected to see Thornfield Hall in all its glory. Instead I saw a ruin[2].

The front of the house was still there. But there was no roof. There were no chimneys, no windows. There was the silence of death there. I understood now why I received no replies to my letters.

What caused this disaster[3]? Did anyone die?

There was no one here to answer these questions. No clue[4] to explain the disaster.

THE DISASTER

- Can you answer Jane's questions?
- What do you think happened at Thornfield Hall?

1 surround [sə`raʊnd] (v.) 圍繞
2 ruin [`rʊɪn] (n.) 斷垣殘壁
3 disaster [dɪ`zæstɚ] (n.) 災難
4 clue [klu] (n.) 線索
5 innkeeper [`ɪn,kipɚ] (n.) 旅館老闆
6 local [`lokḷ] (a.) 當地的
7 inn [ɪn] (n.) 小旅館
8 break out 突然發生
9 discover [dɪs`kʌvɚ] (v.) 發現
10 set fire 縱火
11 dread [drɛd] (v.) 懼怕
12 rescue [`rɛskju] (v.) 營救
13 on foot 步行

The innkeeper[5] of a local[6] inn[7] eventually told me the story.

"It happened last autumn," he said. "After the governess disappeared (but that's another story), Mr Rochester sent his housekeeper and Miss Adela away and shut himself up at the Hall. Then one night a fire broke out[8]. They say it was started by a mad woman who lived in the attic. This woman was later discovered[9] to be Mr Rochester's wife. She managed to set fire[10] to her own room and also to one of the bedrooms on the next floor. Luckily all the servants got out in time but the mad woman went up on the roof. Mr Rochester tried to save her but she jumped off and fell to her death."

"Were there any other deaths?" I asked.

"No," he replied. "But poor Mr Rochester . . ."

"What about him?" I asked, dreading[11] his answer.

"Mr Rochester suffers greatly. A piece of burning wood fell on him and he was badly hurt. He was rescued[12] but he's now blind."

"Where is he? Where does he live now?"

"In a house on one of his farms about thirty miles away. Old John and his wife look after him."

"Will you take me there? I'll pay you well."

"With pleasure, ma'am. And on the way I'll tell you the story of the governess."

"There's no need," I replied. "I know that story already."

When we were a mile from the house, I paid the innkeeper and sent him back. I wanted to arrive on foot[13].

It was early evening and the only sound I could hear was the rain on the leaves.

"Can there be life here?" I asked myself as I approached the house.

Yes, there was. I heard a movement and a figure came out into the evening light and stood on the step. It was a man without a hat. He put his hand out to feel the rain. It was my master, Edward Rochester!

BLINDNESS

- Discuss with a partner and then with the class. Imagine what it is like to be blind.
- Write a list of all the difficulties a blind person might have in everyday life.

I stopped and watched him. I wanted to observe him. He couldn't see me of course because he was blind.

Physically[1], he looked the same as a year ago. He was still a strong man. His back was still straight. His hair was still black. But in his face I could see desperation[2]. He took a few uncertain steps, putting out his arms in front of him to feel his way. Then, defeated[3], he turned and went back into the house.

---

1 physically [ˈfɪzɪklɪ] (adv.) 身體上地
2 desperation [ˌdɛspəˈreʃən] (n.) 絕望
3 defeated [dɪˈfitɪd] (a.) 挫敗的

I waited for a while and then I knocked on the door. Mary, an old servant from Thornfield Hall, opened it. She couldn't believe her eyes when she saw me. I took her hand and followed her into the kitchen. I explained everything to her while we were sitting next to the fire. Then a bell rang. It was Mr Rochester. He wanted some water.

"Give the tray to me," I said. "I'll take it to him."

I was shaking as I went in and my heart was beating fast.

Mr Rochester turned around when he heard the door opening. But because he saw nothing, he turned back and sighed.

I approached him with the glass of water.

"It is you, Mary, isn't it?"

"Mary's in the kitchen," I said.

"Who is this? Who is this?" he demanded. "Answer me! Speak again!" he ordered.

"I arrived only this evening," I said.

"That voice! It's hers! Have I gone mad? Come here! Let me touch you."

I put my hand in his.

"They're her fingers!" he cried. Then he felt my shoulders, my neck, my waist. "Yes! It's her shape, her size. Jane!"

"My dear master," I answered, "I've found you. I've come back to you. I'll never leave you again."

I put my arms around him and kissed his poor eyes.

Then I told him about my new family and my fortune[1] and explained why I went back to Thornfield and how I knew about the fire.

---

1 fortune [ˈfɔrtʃən] (n.) 財產

14. Conclusion

Reader, I married him. We had a quiet but beautiful wedding.

I wrote and told my cousins about it. Diana and Mary were happy for us but St John didn't reply.

I went to see Adela at her school. She was so pleased to see me again. She looked thin and pale and I discovered that the teachers there were very strict. I decided to take her away and put her in another school closer to us. Her new teachers are much kinder and she's doing well in her studies now. We often go and visit her.

I have been married for ten years. I live for my husband and he for me. We talk all day long and never get tired of each other. We are perfectly suited[1] and so live together in complete harmony[2].

For the first two years of our marriage I was Edward's eyes. He saw everything through me. Then one day he told me he could see a little. Following the advice of a doctor in London, he eventually recovered[3] the sight[4] in one eye. It isn't perfect but good enough for him to find his way around. When I put our first baby in his arms, he could see that the child had his eyes— as they were before the fire—large, brilliant[5] and black.

My Edward and I are very happy together. And the happiness of the people we love most makes us even happier.

---

1 suit [sut] (v.) 相配
2 harmony [ˈhɑrmənɪ] (n.) 融洽；和諧
3 recover [rɪˈkʌvɚ] (v.) 恢復
4 sight [saɪt] (n.) 視力
5 brilliant [ˈbrɪljənt] (a.) 明亮的

Ⓐ Personal Response

1 Answer the questions.

ⓐ Did you enjoy reading the story? Why/Why not?

ⓑ Who was your favorite character? Why?

ⓒ Do you think Jane Eyre is passionate and courageous? Why/Why not?

ⓓ What kind of hero do you think Mr Rochester is?

ⓔ Did you guess Mr Rochester was already married to Bertha? Or was it a big surprise?

ⓕ Do you think the ending is realistic? Would you change it? How?

2 *Jane Eyre* was an immediate success when it was published in 1847 but it created a scandal. Can you think why? Discuss with a partner and consider the following:

ⓐ a poor girl who rebels against her guardian;

ⓑ a young girl who advertises for a new job;

ⓒ a governess who falls in love with her employer;

ⓓ a married man who wants to marry another woman;

ⓔ the story is written in the first-person narrative.

Ⓑ Comprehension

3 Tick (✓) true (T) or false (F).

T F ⓐ Jane Eyre enjoyed her childhood at Gateshead Hall and was sad to leave.

T F ⓑ Lowood was an institution, where most of the girls were orphans.

T F ⓒ Mr Brocklehurst humiliated Jane but Miss Temple was kind to her.

T F ⓓ Lowood didn't really change while Jane was there.

T F ⓔ Jane met her employer on the day she arrived at Thornfield Hall.

T F ⓕ Jane disliked Mr Rochester at first but she thought he was very handsome.

T F ⓖ Mr Rochester asked Jane not to talk to the servants about the fire in his room.

T F ⓗ Jane knew about and understood the mystery at Thornfield Hall early in the story.

T F ⓘ Mr Mason stayed at Thornfield Hall for less than 24 hours.

T F ⓙ Mr Rochester was very relaxed on the morning of his wedding to Jane.

T F ⓚ Mr Rochester was forced to marry Bertha by his father—he didn't know she was mad.

T F ⓛ Jane heard about Mr Rochester and his blindness from Mrs Fairfax.

4 Correct the false sentences in Exercise **3**.

5 Match the two parts of the sentences.

1. she didn't learn the truth about it until much later
2. nothing she did satisfied Mrs Reed
3. to make Jane jealous and love him more
4. she wrote to Mr Lloyd to ask him about Jane

_____ a) Jane tried hard to be good for her aunt but
_____.

_____ b) Miss Temple helped Jane clear her name at
Lowood because _____.

_____ c) Jane often heard a strange laugh at Thornfield but
_____.

_____ d) Mr Rochester pretended he wanted to marry Miss
Ingram in order _____.

6 Work with a partner and explain why the following are
important to the story.

a

b

c

ⓒ Characters

7 Tick (✓) the words which can be used to describe Jane.

☐ deceitful
☐ plain
☐ stern
☐ honest
☐ cruel
☐ sincere
☐ daring
☐ courageous
☐ strong

8 In the course of the story the reader witnesses Jane Eyre's growth in character from an unhappy lonely child to a strong young woman. Put the following stages of the development of Jane's character into the correct order.

—— ⓐ Jane is wrongly accused by Mr Brocklehurst and she wants to clear her name.

—— ⓑ Jane tells her aunt, Mrs Reed, what she thinks of her.

—— ⓒ Jane forgives Mrs Reed before she dies.

—— ⓓ Jane studies and works hard at Lowood and eventually becomes a teacher.

—— ⓔ Jane fights back at her cousin's bullying.

—— ⓕ Jane refuses to marry St John because she does not love him.

—— ⓖ Jane is strong and is able to play Mr Rochester's game when he provokes her.

—— [h] Jane loves Mr Rochester but will not stay with him if she cannot be his wife.

—— [i] Jane finds her first job as a governess without anyone's help.

—— [j] Jane goes back to Mr Rochester when she hears he is blind and is now a free man.

—— [k] Jane makes good progress with her pupil Adela.

—— [l] Jane falls in love with Mr Rochester.

9 Complete this paragraph about Mr Rochester with the words in the box.

hero	women	fire
character	element	love

Mr Rochester is an important [a] _____ in the story. He is not your typical romantic [b] _____. He is not handsome and is often moody. This makes him a mysterious character. He is fascinating to [c] _____, as we see with Blanche Ingram and Jane Eyre. He is kind to Adela and to his mad wife, Bertha (he never wants to hurt her and tries to save her in the [d] _____ at the end of the story). We see that he is capable of great [e] _____ through his feelings for and relationship with Jane Eyre. Mr Rochester is an essential [f] _____ in this powerful love story.

10 Put the characters into the correct column.

Mr Brocklehurst
Mrs Fairfax
Diana Rivers
John Reed
Mr Mason
Miss Temple
Blanche Ingram
Bessie
Grace Poole
Mary Rivers
Adela
Helen Burns
Aunt Reed
Bertha
St John Rivers
Mr Rochester

a Gateshead Hall

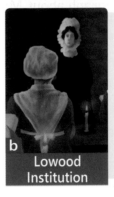
b Lowood Institution

c Thornfield Hall

d Cottage near Whitcross

❹ Plot and Theme

📢 **11** Jane Eyre and her story have strong signs of early feminism. Put the following in the correct order. Then, with a partner, find each episode in the book, and prepare a question and answer session with Jane Eyre about at least two of them.

—— ⓐ Jane advertises and finds her first job as a governess with a good salary.

—— ⓑ Jane returns to Mr Rochester when she is his independent equal—she has her own money and is no longer in his employment.

—— ⓒ Jane wants to be independent and is happy to find a new job when she leaves Thornfield Hall.

—— ⓓ Jane will not become Mr Rochester's mistress.

—— ⓔ Jane studies and works hard to become a governess.

12 Match the different motivations behind these relationships to the couples.

① help with missionary work
② love
③ political or social union
④ money

—— ⓐ Jane Eyre and Mr Rochester
—— ⓑ Mr Rochester and Blanche Ingram
—— ⓒ Mr Rochester and Bertha Rochester
—— ⓓ Jane Eyre and St John Rivers

13 Forgiveness is an important theme in the story. Write down examples of how these characters show signs of forgiveness.

Helen Burns ....

Mr Rochester ....

Jane Eyre ....

14 At the beginning of the story Jane Eyre is a lonely orphan living with cousins who hate her, but by the end Jane's wish for a loving family comes true and she finds some more cousins. Look at this family tree for Jane Eyre. Underline the characters who actually appear in the story.

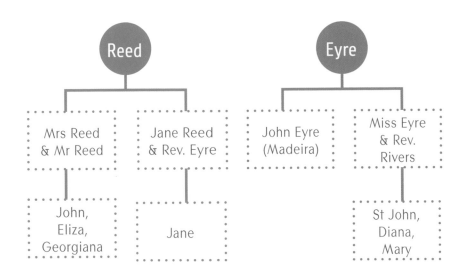

E Language

15 Complete the sentences with the correct form of make/let.

[a] Finally he gave me some of my wages and
_____ me promise to return.

[b] I was determined not to _____ her upset me.

[c] This _____ me cry even harder.

[d] I wanted to walk away calmly but something
_____ me stop and turn round.

[e] Mr Rochester was impatient to get to the church and
_____ me walk so fast that I was out of
breath when we reached the gate.

[f] Helen _____ me feel calm.

[g] He got off the wall to _____ me pass.

16 Bertha Rochester spent most of her adult life locked in an
attic, but she did have a big impact on the story and the
characters. Make a list of all the things Bertha Rochester
managed to do before she died.

Bertha Rochester

She managed to set fire to her
own room and also to one of the
bedrooms on the next floor.

_____

_____

_____

_____

17 Write and then answer questions in the past tense using "How long . . .?" about the following.

(a) Jane Eyre / live / at Gateshead Hall

How long ?

(b) Jane Eyre / stay / at Lowood

How long ?

(c) Jane Eyre / stand / on a stool

How long ?

(d) Jane Eyre / stay / at Gateshead / Aunt Reed's death

How long ?

(e) Jane Eyre / engaged / to Mr Rochester

How long ?

18 Write questions and answers about the following characters using "Why . . . because . . ." Use the adjectives in the box.

sincere
cruel
strange
wicked
humble
obedient
honest
complicated

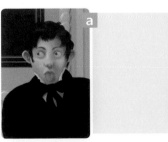
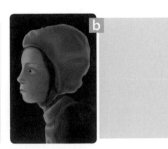

TEST

(76) **1** Listen and tick (✓) the correct picture.

a)
1
2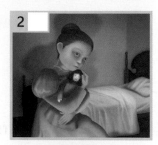

b)
1
2

c)
1
2

d)
1
2

P **2** Tick (✓) true (T) or false (F).

- T F [a] Bessie is the only person who is nice to Jane Eyre at Gateshead Hall.
- T F [b] Mr Brocklehurst makes Jane Eyre stand on a chair at the back of the classroom.
- T F [c] Grace Poole does the cooking and other jobs at Thornfield Hall.
- T F [d] Mr Rochester is really happy to see Mr Mason.
- T F [e] Jane Eyre sees Bertha Rochester twice when she is at Thornfield Hall.
- T F [f] St John Rivers helps Jane find a job as a teacher.
- T F [g] Jane Eyre divides her fortune with her cousins St John, Diana and Mary.
- T F [h] Jane Eyre meets Mr Rochester again at Thornfield Hall.

3 Correct the false sentences.

P **4** Imagine you are Jane Eyre. You are happy to have found Mr Rochester again. Write a letter to your cousins Diana and Mary Rivers. In your letter, you should:

- tell Diana and Mary about your journey to Thornfield Hall;
- say what the innkeeper told you about the disaster;
- say where you are now;
- ask Diana and Mary to visit you.

Write 35–45 words.

Wide Sargasso Sea

The novelist Jean Rhys (1890–1979)
retold Jane Eyre's story through the
character Bertha Rochester (renamed
Antoinette) in her novel *Wide
Sargasso Sea* (1966).

Jean Rhys (1890-1979)

In groups of four do some research on the Internet or in a
library about *Wide Sargasso Sea* and its connection to *Jane
Eyre*. Find information about:

* the novelist Jean Rhys—her life and her reasons
  for writing the novel;
* when and where the novel is set;
* from whose point of view the novel is told
  (who and how many narrators there are);
* how the novel is connected to *Jane Eyre*.

Then make a poster using spidergrams to illustrate your research and:

- find some images (photos, paintings or designs) that you think might represent the novel;
- find some images for *Jane Eyre* and then state how the images for the two books are different;
- state how, after your research, your original opinion of Bertha and Mr Rochester in *Jane Eyre* has changed.

作者簡介　夏綠蒂・勃朗特（Charlotte Brontë, 1816–1855）出生於 1816 年，父親是一位牧師，住在位於約克郡一個小村子哈華斯的牧師公館裡。母親在夏綠蒂五歲時便過世，家中的兄弟姊妹由姨媽所帶大。她和兩個姊姊瑪麗雅、依麗莎白以及妹妹艾蜜莉，曾經上過學校一陣子，然而在 1825 年，瑪麗雅和依麗莎白死於結核病，夏綠蒂於是和艾蜜莉離開學校，由父親在家教導她們和哥哥布倫威爾。

夏綠蒂在英格蘭當過一陣子的家庭教師，後來前往布魯塞爾學習法文，之後留在那裡教書。夏綠蒂返回約克郡後，想和妹妹艾蜜莉、安一起在哈華斯開辦學校，不過因為過於地處偏僻，學校開不成，三姊妹便轉而開始寫作。

1846 年，夏綠蒂說服妹妹們，三人共同出版了《庫瑞、艾里斯和亞克頓・貝爾的詩集》，三姊妹都使用了筆名，因為當時女性的作者並不多見。這本書出版之後，銷售淒慘，不過夏綠蒂在 1847 年出版的《簡愛》，旋即洛陽紙貴。

1854 年，夏綠蒂和牧師尼可拉斯結婚，卻於隔年去世，得年僅 39 歲。

本書簡介　《簡愛》（1847 年出版）的時空背景設定在英國維多利亞時代的約克郡谷地，在那個時代，這本小說並非傳統小說，不過一出版就受到讀者的喜愛，至今不墜。

《簡愛》的故事在講述成長、勇氣和愛，小說描述一位命運悲慘的孤兒女孩，她在成長過程中經歷困難環境，慢慢型塑出簡愛的性格。讀者們可以看到孩提時代個性激烈的簡愛，逐漸變得理性，蛻變為一位成熟、獨立的女性。也因為這個原因，這本小說被視為是教育小說。

小說以主人翁簡愛來作第一人稱敘述，透過這種方式，讀者可以直接觸及簡愛，以及簡愛的心理與行為。簡愛是一個充滿勇氣的女孩，她努力工作，改善自己的條件。在離開佳慈賀府邸冷酷無情的舅媽之後，簡愛進入蘿霧寄宿學校，她學習讓自己成為一位家庭教師，她的第一份工作是在頌芙府邸。不久，簡愛和主人羅哲思德墜入愛河。這份感情顯得糾葛，一方面是因為她的身分是家庭教師，但另一個重要的原因是頌芙府邸閣樓上出現的神祕幽靈。

簡愛並未斬斷這份情緣，不過她也想當一個有尊嚴的獨立女性。簡愛在整部小說中所做出的各種抉擇，在在顯現出她是當時代一位堅強的現代女子，也是文學上最早出現的女性主義典範。小說中處理了許多主題，包括女性在社會、家庭、社會階級以及寬恕中的角色。

第一章　　佳慈賀府邸

P. 15

外面大雨滂沱，天氣冷冽。舅媽瑞德夫人躺在客廳壁爐前的沙發上，她的三個兒女伊萊澤、約翰和喬吉安娜，就圍坐在她旁邊，而她不要我待在那裡。

「簡，等你變得討人喜歡了，再來跟我們坐在一起。」她說：「你現在走開，不可以吵！」

我走進早餐室，從書架上抽下一本書，然後拎著書爬上窗簾後面的窗檯上。

這時，房門突然打開。

「有人在嗎？」約翰‧瑞德大叫道。他停了一下，心想房間裡沒有人。

「跑哪裡去了？」他繼續喊道：「麗茲！喬吉！簡不在這裡！跟媽媽說，她跑去外面淋雨啦！」

房門探進來了伊萊澤的頭，「約翰，她躲在窗簾後面。」

我不想被約翰拖出來，便趕緊現身。

「什麼事？」我問。

P. 16

「你要說，『瑞德少爺，有什麼事嗎？』」約翰回答。他在一張手扶椅上坐下，繼續說道：「你給我過來！」

約翰‧瑞德十四歲，他大我四歲，一直欺負我，我很怕他。在這房子裡，沒有人站在我這邊，僕人們也很怕他，他的母親瑞德夫人視若無睹，我孤立無援。

我朝他的椅子走過去，他對我吐出舌頭。

我知道他想修理我。我盯著他看，心想：「你怎麼這麼醜啊！」

他大概看穿了我的心思，隨即舉起手，狠狠地朝我打下去，我一個跟蹌，從他的椅子前倒退了一、兩步。

「賞你這一下，是因為你對我媽無禮，還有誰教你躲在窗簾後面，而且還這樣瞪著我看——你這個畜牲！」

我知道他想再揍我。

「你幹嘛躲在窗簾後面？」他質問道。

「我在看書。」

P. 17

「把書拿來。」

我走回窗檯旁，把書拿了過來。

「你不是我們家的人，不應該動我們的書。你爸什麼都沒有留給你，你沒有錢，根本沒有資格和我們這種紳士人家的小孩一起住在這裡，跟我們吃一樣的飯，穿我媽買給你的衣服。你拿我的書，我得好好教訓你一下，這些書都是我的。再過不了幾年，這房子裡的所有東西都會變成我的。你現在去門邊站著！」

我照做，結果他把書對準我，丟了過來，我應聲倒下，撞到了頭。我的頭開始流血，因為很痛，我霎時被氣到了。

「惡毒又殘暴的人！你跟殺人犯一樣，跟羅馬暴君一樣！」我說。

「什麼！什麼！伊萊澤、喬吉安娜，你們聽到她說什麼沒？我要去跟我媽講！」

他衝向我，揪住我的頭髮，把我搖來搖去，我憤怒地向他回擊。

「畜牲！畜牲！」他大喊道。

伊萊澤和喬吉安娜跑去找瑞德夫人，等他們回來時，後面還跟了保姆蓓詩和女僕亞伯特小姐。

「你們相信嗎？她竟然攻擊約翰少爺！」我聽到有人說道。

P. 18

　「把她帶到紅色房間去！」瑞德夫人說：「把門反鎖！」

　蓓詩和亞伯特小姐抓住我，我反抗她們，想掙脫開來。

　「亞伯特小姐，抓住她的胳膊！她像隻抓狂的貓！」蓓詩喊道。

　我們進入紅色房間後，她們推著我，讓我坐到一張椅子上。

　「乖乖坐好，不然要把你的手綁起來。」蓓詩說道。

　「我不亂動。」我答應道，一邊用手抓住椅子。

　她們站在那裡看著我，神情嚴肅。

　「小姐，你不要忘了，你虧欠瑞德夫人很多呀，你沒有被送到貧民所，都是因為有夫人在照顧你呀。」蓓詩說。

　我沒有作聲。這些話我並不陌生。

簡

• 對於簡，我們可以得知哪些事情？勾選出正確答案。

☐ 她是一個孤兒。

☐ 她沒有錢。

☐ 她過得不快樂。

☐ 她在她現在住的地方，不受到歡迎。

☐ 她和表兄弟姊妹的關係很好。

☐ 她是宅院裡的僕人。

P. 20

　蓓詩和亞伯特小姐留下我一個人，她們把門帶上，然後反鎖。

　這是一個被閒置的房間，所以裡面很冷。我的舅舅瑞德先生，九年前在這個

房間裡過世，每一個人都認為，在這個房間裡，舅舅陰魂不散。我不記得舅舅這個人，但我知道他是我媽媽的哥哥。我還在襁褓時，父母就過世了，所以瑞德先生就把我帶回家裡。舅舅在過世前，要瑞德夫人承諾會好好照顧我，把我當成親生小孩那樣地對待我。瑞德夫人可能也嘗試過吧，但她無法愛我啊，我又不是她的小孩，而且我長得不漂亮，個性也不開朗。我怎麼可能開朗的起來呢？

　我在紅色房間裡待了一整個夜晚，這實在很恐怖，我滿腦子都是鬼怪和各種聲音，最後嚇昏了過去。

　早上，他們看到我這個樣子，便請羅義德醫生來看我。醫生問了我很多問題，他和藹可親，我就向他說到了殘暴的表哥約翰‧瑞德，還有我自己的不快樂。

　羅義德醫生聽我講我的事情之後，他

問我他可否和瑞德夫人談談。他提出了一個辦法，可以解決大家的問題：瑞德夫人應該把簡・愛送去學校。

我身體很快就恢復，但房子裡沒有半個人來跟我講話，我遭受到了比以前更惡劣的對待。不過，事情開始有了轉變。

P. 21

十一月、十二月和一月的上半月，已經過去了。佳慈賀府邸照例喜氣洋洋地在慶祝耶誕節和新年，人們互相交換禮物，也會有很多的晚餐和晚宴，而我當然是被摒除在所有的歡樂之外的。

晚上，我坐在階梯上，看著表兄弟姊妹在那邊開開心心地嬉戲。之後，我走回冷冷清清的育兒室。我坐下來，凝視著爐火，只有洋娃娃陪我作伴。人總要有個什麼心愛的東西，我心愛的東西是我的洋娃娃。

愛

· 簡說：「人總要有個什麼心愛的東西。」你同意這句話嗎？

· 你心愛的人或心愛的東西是什麼？

會對我好的人就只有蓓詩。在佳慈賀府邸，我最喜歡的人就是她了。一月十五日那一天，就是蓓詩跑上樓，在育兒室裡找到我。

「他們要你去早餐室見他們。」蓓詩急匆匆地說。她把我推到樓梯口，然後自己走回育兒室。

我緩緩走下樓，步入早餐室。舅媽這時坐在爐火邊，她旁邊站了一個高個子的男人，他一身黑衣。

「這就是我寫信跟你提到的小女孩。」瑞德夫人說。

P. 22

那個男人把頭轉向我，打量了我許久。

「小女孩，你叫什麼名字？」他問。

「先生，我叫簡・愛。」我回答。

「那麼，簡・愛，你是個乖小孩嗎？」

「伯寇赫先生，這件事不提也罷。」瑞德夫人幫我回答道。

「哎呀，頑皮的小孩我可不喜歡啊。你知道壞人死掉會去哪裡嗎？」

「會去地獄。」我回答。

「那你早晚有做禱告嗎？」伯寇赫先生繼續問。

「有的，先生。」

「你有在讀《聖經》嗎？」

「有時候會讀。」

「那讚美詩呢？我想你也喜歡吧？」

「我不喜歡，先生。」

P. 23

「不喜歡？這可真令人震驚啊！這顯示你有一顆邪惡的心，你一定要祈禱，祈求上帝改變你的心。」

「伯寇赫先生，我希望你能讓這個小女孩進蘿霧學校。」瑞德夫人插嘴說：「她很愛騙人，會說謊，一定要教她學會謙卑。我想馬上就讓她去上學，讓她待在學校裡，放假時也是。」

伯寇赫先生說：「夫人，這當然可以。你的決定很明智，我們會教導愛小姐學會謙虛和服從。我們學校的女孩都是很謙遜、很懂得順從的。我們蘿霧學校的辦學很成功。」

伯寇赫先生離開之後，我單獨和瑞德夫人在一起。瑞德夫人開始做針線活，我們隻字未談。我很氣她，她說我很愛騙人、會說謊，但我才沒有呢。我盡量要表現良好，可是不管我做什麼，舅媽都不滿意。她就是不讓我好過。

不一會兒，她從手上的活兒抬起頭來。「回育兒室去。」她說。

我站起身來，等我走到門口時，我停下腳步，又掉頭走回來，我一定要跟她說個清楚！我深深吸了一口氣。

「我才沒有騙人，也沒有說謊！我不會說我愛你，因為我才不愛你呢！在這個世界上，我最討厭的人，除了約翰‧瑞德，就是你！會說謊的是你女兒喬吉安娜，才不是我！」

瑞德夫人瞪著我看。

「我再也不會叫你舅媽了！」我繼續說：「我要跟別人說你是怎麼對待我的，說你是怎麼欺負我的。」

「簡‧愛，你怎麼敢說這種話！」

「我怎麼敢？瑞德夫人，我怎麼敢？因為這是事實！你以為我沒有感覺，你以為我沒有人愛、沒有人關心，也可以活下去，但是我不行！你一點仁慈心都沒有，你可惡的兒子打我，你卻把我鎖在紅色房間裡。以後只要有人問我，我就會把事情都抖出來。大家都以為你是一個好人，事實上你又壞又卑鄙，你才是會騙人的人！」

第二章　蘿霧學校

幾天後，蓓詩早早就把我叫起床，我那天早上要離開佳慈賀府邸了。只有蓓詩送我上馬車，瑞德夫人並不想看到我。

我穿過大廳，走出前門時，我喊道：「再會了！」我很高興就要離開了，我一心想展開我的新生活。

蓓詩抱住我，親吻了我一下。

「好好照顧她。」護送的人幫忙讓我坐上馬車時，她對他說道。

這裡到蘿霧有五十英里遠，馬車一趟要走很久，於是我睡著了。

等馬車停下來時，我才醒過來，這時已經是晚上時分了。一個像是僕人的人站在馬車的門邊。

「這裡有一位叫簡‧愛的小女孩嗎？」那人問道。

「有。」我回答。

護送的人抱起我，將我放到地上，旁邊是我的大行李箱。之後馬車旋即駛離。

我環顧了一下，四周飄著風雨，一片漆黑。女僕帶我穿進一棟大房子的門。大廳裡有一位高個子的女士來接我，她看起來像是重要人物。在她的身後，站了另一位女士。

之後米勒小姐帶我離開。這房子很大，她帶我一路經過很多各式各樣的房間，我可以聽到遠遠傳來的講話嗡嗡聲。最後，我們走進一個長型的房間裡。各種年紀的女孩坐在長桌兩旁的長木椅上，其中年紀最小的約莫九歲、十

歲，最大的是二十歲。她們都穿著相同的棕色毛質連身裙，綁著白色圍兜。她們正在讀書，嗡嗡的話語聲是女孩們各自反覆讀誦課文的聲音。桌邊坐著的女孩們，彷彿多得數不盡，但我後來知道蘿霧學校共有八十位女孩。

米勒小姐要我在門邊的一張長椅上坐下，然後她走到長型房間的最前面。

「班長，把書收走！」她大聲喊道。

四位高個子的女孩便將女孩們桌上的書本收走。

「班長，把晚餐托盤拿來！」米勒小姐喊道。

P. 28

高個子的女孩們將托盤上的一份份食物分發出去，但我沒有胃口，我太亢奮又太累了。

晚餐結束時，米勒小姐唸了禱告文，之後所有的女孩便走上樓，來到另一間擺滿床的長型房間裡。每一張床睡兩個女孩，而我那一晚和米勒小姐睡。我一下子就睡著了，累得連作夢也沒有。

學校

- 簡對學校的第一個印象是什麼？
- 她的學校和你的學校有什麼不一樣？和夥伴們討論。

隔天早上，轟耳的鈴響聲叫醒了我們。這時曙光未現，非常寒冷，我連忙穿上衣服。鈴聲又響了一次，我們大家都來到樓下的教室裡。

米勒小姐唸過禱告文，然後喊道：「分班！」

我們各自在不同的班級裡，讀了一個多小時的《聖經》。之後，我們魚貫進入另一個房間裡用早餐。我飢腸轆轆，可是我們眼前的食物味道卻很可怕。

「噁！粥又煮焦了！」一個女孩小聲説道。

「安靜！」一個老師喊道。

我很快動手吃飯，但才吃了一口，我就打住了，真難以下嚥啊！我看了看旁邊的人，每一個人的湯匙都扒得很慢。

P. 29

我看到每個女孩都在試嚐粥的味道，想把粥吞下去，但是絕大多數人在嚐過之後也都作罷了。

等早餐的結束鈴聲響起時，大家還是空著肚子。

我看到一位老師試了一下粥的味道，「真噁心！真該罵！」她對另一個老師小聲説道。

我們走回教室，再一次分班。上課前，大家先起立，昨晚那位高個子、看起來像是重要人物的女士，這時步入了教室。我後來知道她的名字是田普小姐，她是蘿霧學校的校長，負責教導年紀較長的女孩。

中午十二點的鐘聲響起之際，校長站起來，說道：「今天早上，你們的早餐都沒有吃，大家一定很餓了，我已經吩咐給你們大家準備麵包加起司的午餐。」

老師們看著她，露出吃驚的表情。

「我會負起這個責任。」她說完這句話之後，便走出教室。

我們大家於是開心地吃了麵包和起司，然後來到外面的花園裡。

P. 30

身體強健的女孩，她們奔來跑去地嬉戲著，蒼白瘦弱的女孩則擠在一起互相取暖，她們當中有一些人咳得很厲害。

我獨自一人站著，沒有人和我講話，不過我並不覺得孤單或難過。對我來說，孤伶伶一個人是很正常的。我抬頭望了望學校的建築，看著石板上刻著的文字：

蘿霧學校
本大樓由伯寇赫府邸的
納蜜·伯寇赫所建

當我正在想「institution」這個字是什麼意思時，我聽到身後傳來了咳嗽聲。我轉身，看到有個女孩正坐在石椅上看著書。

「你的書好看嗎？」我問她。

「我是滿喜歡的。」她答道，小心地看著我。

「你可以跟我說『institution』這個字是什麼意思嗎？」我問。

「這是說，這間學校是半慈善性質的學校。我們都是慈善學校的小孩，我想你和我們大家一樣，也是孤兒吧？」她說。

「我是。」我說。

「那納蜜·伯寇赫又是誰？」我問道，想了解更多。

「這棟房子新蓋的部分，就是她蓋的。她已經過世了，現在學校歸她兒子管。」

P. 31

「那麼說，這個大樓不是那個高個子女士的？就是吩咐準備麵包加起司的那位女士。」

「你是說田普小姐？哦，很可惜，不是。她是伯寇赫先生雇用的人。」

伯寇赫先生

•你記得伯寇赫先生嗎？翻回第 22 頁看看。

「他住在這裡嗎？」我問。

「沒有，他和他家人住在兩英里外的一棟大房子裡。他是一位牧師。」

「你喜歡這裡的老師嗎？」

「他們滿好的。」

「你來這裡多久了？」

「兩年。你問太多了，我要看書。」她對我說。

就在這時，晚餐的鈴聲響起，我們得進屋了。

第三章　　海倫·本斯

P. 32

我不久就得知了新朋友的名字，因為有一位老師老是在挑她的毛病。

「本斯，站好！」她說。（這裡的老師都是稱呼我們的姓）或是，「本斯，不要那樣看我！」

有一天，她被罰要站在教室的中間，以示大眾。

本斯班上女孩的考試，她全都會作答。在班上的女孩中，她懂得最多，不過那位老師從不誇獎她。

「本斯，你的指甲怎麼這麼髒！」老師只會這樣叨念她。

我搞不懂老師為什麼要懲罰她，她又沒有做錯事情。不過，她每次被懲罰或是被罵時，都不會生氣。老師常說她的不是，但是她都不會反駁。即使老師用棍子打她，她也是照樣一副沉靜、卑微的樣子，而我只看過她哭過一次。

晚間時刻，我們有一整個鐘頭的休息時間。一天晚上，我看到本斯坐在爐火邊，讀著之前就在讀的那本書。我走過去，在她旁邊坐下來。

「本斯，你叫什麼名字？」我問她。

「海倫。」她答道。

「你想離開蘿霧嗎？」

「我不想。為什麼要離開？我是被送來這裡受教育的啊。」

「可是老師對你很壞！」

P.34

「很壞？一點也不會啊，那是嚴厲，我有什麼缺點，她就指正。」

「可是她打你耶，你又不是壞女孩！」我喊道：「你這麼聰明，怎麼都不會對她生氣呢？她要是打我，我不會默不吭聲。」

「你只能接受啊，學生如果不服從紀律，會被伯寇赫先生開除。我們要服從

紀律，不要造成別人的困擾。《聖經》教導我們去愛我們的敵人，以德報怨。」海倫回答說。

真難以置信，海倫怎麼能夠這麼寬恕別人？她沒有犯錯，老師卻打她，那個老師很殘暴，脾氣很壞。

「田普小姐也會對你這麼壞嗎？」我問。

「哦，不會，田普小姐的人很好。我犯錯時，她也會跟我講。犯錯是很不好的，我一定要學習做一個更好的人。你還小，以後也會學到這一點的。」她回答。

我開始說道：「可是海倫，如果有人對我不好，或是沒有道理的懲罰我，我會討厭他們，這是很自然的啊。就像別人對你好，你就會喜歡他們；自己真的犯錯了，就會接受懲罰。」

我看得出來海倫並不同意我的話。那天晚上，我們沒再交談過。

對懲罰的看法

· 你同意誰的看法，海倫的還是簡的？為什麼？和夥伴討論。

第四章　伯寇赫先生

P.35

我在蘿霧度過的第一個冬天，又長又難熬。今年的雪很多，天寒地凍的，我們穿的衣服根本不夠禦寒，而且被分配的食物很少，大家都一直處在饑寒交迫的狀態中。

不過對我來說，這個冬天更慘的事情，是我在學校第一次碰到伯寇赫先生到來時所發生的情況。

在我來蘿霧不久後的一個午後，教室裡走進來一個高大的黑衣人物，我很快認出來那是伯寇赫先生。大家停下在寫字板上寫字的動作，起身站立，連老師也站直身子。我很不安，伯寇赫先生從瑞德夫人那裡聽來不實的消息，我知道他想跟大家說我會編謊話。

他跟田普小姐談到校務，碎碎唸了一大堆事情，像是女孩們吃的東西太多啦，衣服洗得太勤啦，有的女孩的頭髮不夠直啦，甚至還唸說有一些女孩長得太高啦。田普小姐按捺住性子，聽他胡亂怪罪一通。

P.36

這期間，我都把臉藏在我的寫字板後面，不想讓伯寇赫先生看到，未料我因為害怕，反而讓寫字板掉下來，摔到了地板上，裂成碎片。每個人都轉身看著我。

伯寇赫先生說：「啊，是那個新來的女孩！她的事情，我可要說說了。女孩，你過來。」

我身邊的女孩們把我推向前，有兩個班長把我抱到凳子上。凳子擺在教室的正中間，每一個人都盯著我看。

「各位女孩！各位老師！你們大家都看到了這個女孩吧？她還很小，也很健康，但是我一定要警告你們，她很邪惡，而且很會說謊！這是她的恩人瑞德夫人告訴我的，那位好心的女士待她不薄，但是這個女孩會騙人，很不老實。瑞德夫人把這個女孩送到這裡來，讓她學習變乖、變誠實。各位老師，你們務必好好管教她，她不乖時，就要好好懲戒她。各位女孩！你們千萬不要跟她玩，也不要和她講話，我們大家應該都要想辦法來拯救她的靈魂。現在，就讓她在凳子上再罰站半個小時吧。」

伯寇赫先生說完這些話，就走出教室。

這個懲罰實在太不公平了，我很憤怒，覺得受到羞辱。我雙頰漲紅，呼吸不順暢，無法目視任何人。

P.37

但是後來，有一個人從我身邊走過，是海倫·本斯。當她又再次從我身邊走過時，她抬眼看我，對我笑了一下。她的笑容，至今仍留在我的腦海裡！這給了我力量，我站在凳子上，抬高了頭。

羞辱

· 為什麼簡所受到的懲罰是不公平的？

· 你有過被羞辱的感覺嗎？和夥伴討論。

五點的鐘聲響起，半個小時過去了，我爬下凳子，走到已空無一人的教室角落裡，開始哭了起來。我努力要在蘿霧學校表現良好，讓自己有一個新的開始。我的學業表現很好，老師們都喜歡我，可是現在大家都以為我是個會說謊的人了，一想到這裡，我哭得更厲害了。

這時海倫出現了。她從餐廳幫我帶了一些咖啡和麵包過來，可是我什麼都不想吃、不想喝。我繼續哭著，海倫在我旁邊坐了下來。

我先開口說話，「海倫，你為什麼要來陪我？每個人都認為我是個會說謊的人，大家都討厭我。」

P. 38

「他們才不討厭你呢，大家都很同情你。」海倫回答說：「沒有人喜歡伯寇赫先生，只要你繼續這樣乖乖的，大家很快就會把他講的話都忘光光。你會發現，大家冷淡的態度很快就會變好了。」

我沒有回話，海倫讓我安靜了下來。我把頭依偎在她的肩膀上，雙手抱著她，一直到有人走過來時，我還抱著她。那是田普小姐。

「簡·愛，我是來找你的，我想和你談一談。海倫·本斯，你也可以一起過來。」

我們跟著田普小姐來到她的房間，然後她要我們坐下來。

「你哭好了嗎？」田普小姐望著我的臉，問道。

「還沒。」我回答。

「是怎麼樣嗎？」

「我是被誣告的，而女士您，還有其他每一個人，大家現在都會認為我很壞。」

「簡，那麼我想聽聽你的說法囉，跟我說說你的事吧，我想知道真實的情況。」

田普小姐親切地說道。

於是，我便跟田普小姐說了我自己的事。我盡量把所有的事情都說出來，也把所有相關的人的名字都講出來。我還講了自己的缺點，並且努力壓抑住自己怨恨的情緒。

P. 40

田普小姐靜靜地看著我好一會兒，最後說道：「我認識羅義德先生，就你說的那位醫生。我會寫信給他，如果你們兩個人所說的話是一樣的，我會公開針對每一項指控，還給你清白。不過對我來說呢，簡，你現在已經是清白的了。」

田普小姐一邊說著這些仁慈的話，一邊親吻了我。之後，她轉向海倫。

「海倫，你今晚的咳嗽還好嗎？」

「有好一點點了。」海倫回答。

田普小姐接著叫來了茶和土司。那天晚上，我們享受了滿滿的食物、溫暖、仁慈和溫情。

一個星期之後，田普小姐收到了羅義德醫生的回信。他表示，我說的話都是真的。當天，田普小姐就當眾對著每一個人宣布，伯寇赫先生對簡·愛所做的指控，都不是真的。老師們親吻了我，同伴們也都給了我微笑，我好開心啊。

第五章 病倒

P. 41

我重獲清白了。我在學業上很用功，後來被升到較高的班級，並且開始學習法語和繪畫。

春天來了，帶來了溫暖的氣候，但卻

也帶來了斑疹傷寒。五月時，有很多女孩發高燒，蘿霧學校的一部分變成了醫院。

食物少，再加上嚴重的咳嗽和感冒，學生們變得虛弱。在學校的八十個女孩當中，就有四十五個人生病了。班級常停課，紀律也放鬆了，因為老師們都忙著照顧生病的學生。有一些女孩被送回家，以防染病，或是回家等待臨終。也有一些人在學校裡病逝了。

蘿霧這個地方現在顯得更陰鬱了，而且瀰漫著恐懼。只有走到屋外的花園裡，才能稍微得到喘息，在那裡才能感受到春日花暖，也可以在林間漫步。

我身體無恙，可是我的摯友海倫·本斯就不然了。她被送到樓上的房間，我不能去看她。我常常想到她，也常常跟老師詢問她的狀況。有一次，我聽到這樣的回答：「她跟我們在一起的時間不會太久了。」

我聽得懂這是指死亡，而不是說要送她回家。我一定要在她死去之前，再見她一面。

P. 42

一位護士跟我說，她現在在田普小姐的房間裡，於是我便前去找她。

她躺在帷幕後的床上。

「海倫，你醒著嗎？」我小聲地輕輕說道。

「是你嗎，簡？」她用她甜美的聲音問道。

我爬上她的床，親吻了她。她的身子又瘦又冰冷。

「海倫，我來看你了。」

「你來跟我說再見，我想你趕上時間了。」

「海倫，你會去哪裡？你會回家嗎？」

「會，我會回去我最後的家。」

「不要！海倫，不要！」我喊道。

「簡，陪我，不要離開我！」海倫說：「我很開心喔，我要去上帝那裡了，他很愛我。簡，抱我。」

「海倫，晚安，我不會離開你，我會跟你在一起。」

她親吻了我，我也親吻了她，之後我們一起入睡了。

那天晚上，海倫在我的臂彎裡，走了。

很多女孩死於高燒，有一些人開始提出質疑。他們很快發現學校的環境很惡劣，非著手改變不可。伯寇赫先生不再有那麼多支配權，人們成立了委員會來負責做決策。這些改變都是有利於我們學生，環境變得比較舒適，對學生的關懷變得比較多，更關鍵的是，食物也變多了。這個學校開始逐步變成一間真正有益的學校了。

P. 44

我之後在蘿霧又待了八年之久：有六年是當學生，有兩年是當老師。在這八年裡，我在學業或工作上都很認真，也學到了很多東西。田普小姐——她是我的母親、我的老師，後來也成了我的朋友——她後來結婚，離開了學校。我很想念她，我開始思索自己是否也該離開蘿霧了。

對於未來要怎麼做，我想了很多、很久。最後，我決定在報紙上登廣告：

「年輕女士，尋找私人家庭女教師的職位，兒童年齡在十四歲以下。

足勝任所有通識科目的教學，包括法語、繪畫和音樂。」

幾天後，我收到了一封來信：

「某私人家庭需要一名女教師，教導一名未滿十歲的小女孩，年薪三十英鎊。請將推薦函和詳細資料寄至彌蔻特附近的頌芙，收信人為斐法夫人。」

P. 46

我仔細讀了信件，很期待這是一份好工作、一個好人家。我孤身在世，找不到人給我建議。

我跟校長提及這份工作，也說到薪水頗佳。我也請她跟伯寇赫先生和委員會提這件事，我想請他們寫推薦函。

伯寇赫先生說，我應該要先徵得瑞德夫人的同意，因為她是我法定的監護人。於是我寫了信給她，並得到了回函，她表示我可以自行決定。委員會終於允許我離開，並給了我所需的推薦信。

現在，我一切就緒，即將成為頌芙府邸的家庭教師。

改變

・你想簡為什麼想離開蘿霧學校？
・你想她是什麼樣的心情？
・你想簡是一位有志向的人嗎？
・你是有志向的人嗎？和夥伴討論。

第六章　頌芙府邸

P. 47

前往彌蔻特的車程要十六個鐘頭，我有很多時間去猜想我的新東家斐法夫人，但願她不是另一個瑞德夫人！當我抵達時，有一輛馬車正等著載我前往頌芙府邸。

兩個小時後，馬車在一棟長型的大宅前停下。一個女孩打開大門，我走了進去。

她領我來到一間舒適的小房間，裡面燒著爐火，令人感到愉快，旁邊坐著一位個子嬌小的老婦人，正在織著毛衣。

「親愛的，一切可好？」她一邊說，一邊起身迎接我，「這趟路程很遠，快來爐火邊，你一定很冷吧。」

「您是斐法夫人嗎？」我問。

「是的，請坐。」

她幫我脫下帽子和披巾，並且要女孩先把衣物拿去我的房間。

「然後再幫愛小姐拿點吃的過來。」她說。

「她待我如賓客。」我心想，我沒料到會有一個這麼親切的東家。

P. 48

「我今晚有幸可以見到斐法小姐嗎？」我問。

「斐法小姐？喔，你是說華倫小姐，雅德蕾・華倫，這是你學生的名字。」

「喔，那她不是您的女兒？」

「不是，我沒有家人。我很高興你來這裡，頌芙的冬天可寂寞了。我之前只有僕人可以聊天，不過現在有雅德蕾、有保姆，還有你也來了，以後我們大家可以快快樂樂地在一起了。」

斐法太太繼續聊著，我一邊吃著東西。我愈來愈喜歡她了。

當晚，我睡得很香甜。斐法太太很親切，我的房間舒適又溫暖。

隔天早上，我睜開眼時，天光已亮。陽光灑進來，房間看起來很溫馨，和我在薄霧的房間完全不同。

「我會喜歡在這種地方工作的。」我心情愉快地想著。

我穿好衣服，開始探索。樓下的前門開著，我步出大門，來到花園。這是一個怡人的秋日，遠望過去，是林子和山丘。我欣賞著這片景色，呼吸著清新的空氣。這時，門口邊出現了斐法太太。

「你還喜歡頌芙嗎？」她問。

我跟她說，我很喜歡這裡。

「是啊，這地方很美，羅哲思德先生應該多花一點時間待在這裡的。」她說。

「羅哲思德先生？他是誰？」我嚷道。

「他就是頌芙府邸的主人，你不知道嗎？」她答道。

「我還以為頌芙府邸是你的。」

「我的？親愛的孩子，這可異想天開了，我只是個管家呀。」

羅哲思德先生

· 你想羅哲思德先生可能是個什麼樣的人？
· 列出至今所知道的訊息。當你一路閱讀本書時，把新的訊息加上去。

「那麼，那位小女孩、我的學生，她是？」

「羅哲思德先生是她的監護人，是先生要我幫她找家庭教師的。你看，她和保姆過來了。」

一個有著一頭長捲髮的漂亮小女孩往我們這邊走過來。

「早啊，雅德蕾小姐，跟愛小姐打個招呼吧，她是來教你讀書的，要讓你變成一位聰慧的淑女。」斐法太太說。

「早安。」雅德蕾說。她轉過頭，用法語向身後的保姆問了一個問題。

「她會說英語嗎？」我問斐法太太。

「會一點點，不過她的保姆蘇菲就完全不會講英語了。」斐法太太說。

我慶幸我的法語講得還不錯，而雅德蕾也很高興看到我會講她的語言。

「你的法語講得和羅哲思德先生一樣好！」她驚呼道。

她跟我說，她母親過世後，羅哲思德先生就帶著她和蘇菲，從法國坐著一艘大船來到英國，然後在頌芙住了下來。不過羅哲思德先生現在不住這裡，也都沒有來看她。

早餐過後，雅德蕾和我來到圖書室。這裡就是我們的教室，裡面有圖書、一個地球儀、一架鋼琴，還有一個畫架。

我們一直上課到上中午，然後再把雅德蕾交回給蘇菲。我打算利用那個下午來畫一些東西，明天幫雅德蕾上課時可以使用。於是，我走上樓去拿一些紙筆。

當我走上樓梯時，斐法太太從她正在打掃的房間裡，叫住了我。

「我猜你早上的課上完了吧？」

我走下樓梯，和她講話。這個房間很大，有紫色的椅子、紫色的窗簾，地板鋪著土耳其地毯。

P.52

「好漂亮的房間！」我一邊叫道，一邊環顧房間，「你打掃得真乾淨！」

「是啊，羅哲思德先生是很少回來，可是都是突然無預期地回來。他常會帶客人回來，所以我都會把一切打點好，等他回來。」

「羅哲思德先生是一個什麼樣的人？」我問。

「他是個紳士，也是一個好主人，大家都敬愛他。他很聰明，只是有點兒怪怪的。」

「怎樣怪怪的？」

「我也不知道，説不上來，你很難看得出來他是快樂還是不快樂。」

斐法太太隨後帶我看過整棟宅第樓上樓下的所有房間。最後，她帶我步出閣樓，來到屋頂上。

P.53

「從這裡看過去的景色真美。」她說。

在秋天明亮的陽光下，花園和田野看起來很美，等我們再進到屋子裡，閣樓就顯得特別陰暗。突然，這時傳來了一個奇怪的聲音，那是一個低沉的笑聲。我停下腳步聆聽，又聽到了一聲。

「你有聽到笑聲嗎？是誰在笑？」我問斐法太太。

「我想是僕人吧，大概是葛麗絲·普爾。」

P.54

這時又傳來了聲音。

「葛麗絲！」斐法太太喊道。

一個閣樓房間的門被打開來，走出來一個婦女。她年約四十歲，有一頭紅髮，長相一般。

「葛麗絲，太吵囉，要記住給你的吩咐。」斐法太太説。

婦女不發一語地點頭，然後走回房裡。

「葛麗絲在這裡工作，做女紅之類的活兒。」斐法太太跟我説：「跟我説説吧，你的學生雅德蕾小姐今天早上的表現如何呀？」

我瞬間忘掉葛德絲·普爾的事，我們一邊聊著雅德蕾，一邊來到樓下。

猜一猜

· 為什麼葛麗絲·普爾要待在閣樓裡工作？

· 她要謹記什麼樣的吩咐？

第七章　羅哲思德先生

P.55

我在頌芙府邸過得很愉快，斐法太太是一位親切、沉著又明理的人，我的學生是一個活潑熱情的孩子，她努力要討我歡心。一開始，她並不好教，因為她被寵壞啦，不過她很快就變得乖巧，學業上也進步很多。

我在頌芙府邸的生活無可挑剔，只是常常覺得有點無聊。我唯一的抒發方式就是走走路，有時是逛逛花園，有時是在三樓的走廊上踱步，有時是在屋頂上漫步。

我在三樓時，常會聽到葛麗絲·普爾的笑聲。有些日子她很安靜，有些日子又可以聽到她大笑的聲音。我遇到她時，有時候會和她講話，可是她並不想開口，只是走回她閣樓的房間裡。

十月、十一月、十二月，轉眼已過。一月時，雅德蕾得了感冒，我們暫時休課。為了打發午後的閒暇時間，我提議要步行到兩英里外的黑鎮，去幫斐法太太寄信。那天很冷，我快步走路，好讓身體保持暖和。

我走了快一半的路程時，傳來一陣奔馳的馬蹄聲，劃破了寧靜。我停下腳步，讓馬匹先過。

不一會兒，傳來很大聲的摔落聲音，我便跑回頭去看看是怎麼一回事。

P.56

馬匹和騎士都摔在了地上。

「先生，你有受傷嗎？」我問。

那個人沒有作聲，於是我又問了一次：「需要幫忙嗎？」

「請讓開。」他回答。

他年紀約莫三十五歲，一頭黑髮，膚色黝黑，長得不是說很帥。但我倒不怕他，也不會覺得彆扭。事實上，他生氣的表情反倒讓我看了滿喜歡的，所以我沒有讓開。

「先生，我不能就這樣丟下你，天色晚了，你只有自己一個人，我一定要看到你騎上馬，我才可以離開。」我說。

我一邊說著，他一邊注視著我，他到這個時候才正眼瞧了我。

「你怎麼不是待在家裡頭？你住哪裡？」他問我。

「我住在頌芙，現在要去黑鎮寄信。」我回答。

「頌芙的主人是誰？」

「是羅哲思德先生。」

「你認識羅哲思德？」

「不認識，我沒見過他。」

「你顯然不是府邸的僕人，你是……」，他打住，目光掠過我的穿著，似乎是在想我為什麼要這樣幫他。

P.58

「我是家庭教師。」

「喔，家庭教師！」他重覆說道，「當然，就是家庭教師了！」

他想站起來，可是他的腳疼得厲害。

「你不用去找人來幫忙，不過如果你願意，你可以幫我一點忙。」他說。

「當然，先生。」

「把我的馬帶過來。」

我想牽住馬，但是馬很躁動，我抓住不牠。男人在那裡等著，觀看了一會兒，不禁笑了起來。

「我明白了，馬如果不過來，那就換我

過去吧。請來扶我一下。」他說。

他把手搭在我的肩膀上，慢慢走向馬匹。他三兩下就牽住了馬，跳上馬背，儘管他的腳踝在發疼。看得出來，他的騎術很好。

騎士

・你想這個騎士是誰？

「謝謝！去黑鎮寄信吧，快去快回。」

他奔馳而去，他的一隻狗跟在後面追跑著。

P. 59

我在黑鎮寄出了信，然後返回頌芙。天色漸自暗了，我在剛才遇到騎士、伸手相助的地方，佇足了一會兒。

這件插曲也不是什麼大事情，卻激盪了我的一些思緒。這是一張陌生的面孔、一段新的記憶，我不想直接返回頌芙，不想讓這段回憶被淹沒在安穩而一成不變的生活中。

等我最後推開頌芙府邸的大門，步入屋內時，已經夜幕低垂。我聽到餐廳傳來講話聲，我認出其中有雅德蕾的聲音。我前往斐法太太的房間，看到壁爐前坐著一隻狗，那隻狗的樣子跟那位騎士的狗很相像。

我叫了一個僕人過來問，「這狗是誰的？」

「牠是跟主人羅哲思德先生一起回來的狗。先生剛回來，他現在正在餐廳跟大家一起用餐。約翰去請醫生了，因為主人出了一點意外，他的馬摔跤，他扭到了腳踝。」

「我知道了。」我說。

我拿起燭台，先上樓去換衣服，再下來用餐。

P. 60

那天晚上，我並未再見到羅哲思德先生，他聽從醫生的囑咐，早早上了床。

第二天，宅院裡開始忙著搬移、張羅東西，而且多了很多的人氣。

雅德蕾也顯得很興奮，她告訴我說：「羅哲思德先生給我帶了禮物，禮物就他的箱子裡。」她說。

向晚時分，屋子裡才安靜下來一些，斐法太太來到我的房間。

「羅哲思德先生請你和雅德蕾等一會兒去客廳和他用茶，你換件衣服吧，我來幫你。」她說。

「有需要換嗎？」我問。

「有啊，羅哲思德先生待在頌芙時，我都是這樣的。」她回答。

P. 61

爐火旁，雅德蕾已經坐定在羅哲思德先生的腳邊。我們走進客廳時，羅哲思德先生並沒有抬起頭來招呼我們，所以我們就靜靜地坐下，等他開口。斐法太太想開話匣子，但是他既不說話，也沒有做出什麼動作。茶點送進來時，我和雅德蕾移身到桌旁，但他仍坐在沙發上。

「請把羅哲思德先生的茶端過去。」斐法太太一邊說，一邊把他的茶杯遞給我。

「你也有準備愛小姐的禮物嗎？」羅哲思德先生從我手中接過茶杯時，雅德蕾問道。

「禮物？」羅哲思德先生一邊說，一邊

轉過臉來看著我，這還是他在這屋子裡第一次注視我。「愛小姐，你有想說我會帶禮物給你嗎？」

「沒有想過，先生。您不認識我，況且無功不受祿。」我回答。

「那倒未必，你把雅德蕾教得很好，她功課進步很多。」羅哲思德先生回答。

「先生，那這就是您給的禮物了，給教師的最好禮物，就是讚美他的學生進步很多。」我說。

「哼！」羅哲思德先生說罷，便靜靜地喝起茶來。

茶喝完，他說：「到爐火邊來吧。」

他開始問起蘿霧的事，還有我的家庭狀況。之後，他要我彈首鋼琴曲子，還要我給他看我的畫作。顯然，他是在測試我，他想激怒我，看我會有什麼反應。

P.62

不過，我夠強韌的，可以奉陪。我用我平常跟他講話的口氣，禮貌得體地一一回答他的問題。

終於，大夥兒讓他感到累了，他便打發我們去睡覺。

激怒

• 你容易被激怒嗎？
• 人們激怒你時，你的反應如何？

「我覺得羅哲思德先生脾氣古怪，個性複雜。」我之後跟斐法太太說道。

「大概吧，不過我們不要跟他計較，除了是個性使然，也是因為他有很多問題。」

「什麼樣的問題？」我問。

「家庭問題。這個大宅院牽扯到很多人，我想這也是他這麼久以來都不待在頌芙的原因吧。」

我想了解多一點，但斐法太太的表情明白顯示她不想再繼續聊他的事情。

第八章　大火

P.63

接下來幾天，我沒怎麼見到羅哲思德先生。他老是忙著，不然就是騎馬外出。

一天晚上，用過晚餐後，他請人來叫我和雅德蕾過去。他心情很好，給了雅德蕾一直在期待的禮物。

「去別的地方打開禮物吧，不要再來吵我囉。」他說。

接著，他轉身向我，說道：「愛小姐，請過來坐在這邊，這樣我就不用調整我在這張舒適椅子上的坐姿，也能看到你。」

他坐著，凝視爐火好一會兒，讓我有時間可以端詳他。他有一雙大眼睛，黑色的眸子，很漂亮，而且眼神深邃。

「愛小姐，你在打量我。」他看著我說：「你覺得我帥嗎？」

「不帥，先生。」我不假思索地回答。

「哈，哈！」他笑道：「愛小姐，你是個很不一樣的女孩，你看起來很正經，安安靜靜的，可是一回答起問題來，可真是直言不諱啊！」

P.65

我覺得很不好意思，想跟他道歉，不過他倒是喜歡我的直率。那天晚上，我們聊了許久。我明白到，他為過去所犯的一個錯誤而感到自責,他現在很懊悔,渴望自己能成為一個比較好的人。此外,他也想追尋快樂。

在我們深談之後不久的一個午後,那時我正和雅德蕾待在戶外,羅哲思德先生突然出現。雅德蕾開始和他的狗玩耍,我便和羅哲思德先生繞著花園散步。他聊到他的過去,還有雅德蕾的事。

他說:「她是巴黎一個舞蹈家的女兒。她叫色鈴·華倫,我和她有過一段情,不過她欺騙了我的感情,和另一位追求者去了義大利,把女兒雅德蕾丟在巴黎。她說我是女兒的父親,但我知道我不是。我並不知道她的父親是誰,這可憐的小女孩無依無靠,我就伸出援手。我不知道自己幹嘛要告訴你這些事情,希望你不會因為知道了這些內情,就轉而求去。這些事讓你震驚吧?」

「並沒有,現在知道這些事情,只會讓我更加疼愛雅德蕾。」我回答。

就這樣,我逐漸和羅哲思德先生建立起友誼。他不會那麼陰陽怪氣了,而且會常常找我講話。我們的交談讓我感到快樂,而且填補了我生命中的缺憾。

跟他在一起,我覺得很有活力。他盡量讓自己變得好相處一些,只不過,他臉上總是帶著一股莫名的哀傷,似乎對我藏著什麼不為人知的事。

P. 66

哀傷

- 人生中什麼樣的境遇會讓人哀傷?
- 羅哲思德先生那股莫名的哀傷,有可能是什麼原因造成的?

那天夜晚,我躺在床上琢磨著羅哲思德先生的事。「他會很快就離開頌芙嗎?」我心想,「斐法太太說過,他從不久留的,而他這次已經待了八個星期了。他要是離開了,這個宅院會變成一個讓人傷心的地方。」

這時,我突然聽一個奇怪的聲音,好像是從樓上傳下來的,我坐起身來,心跳急促。時鐘這時敲響了兩聲,有人或有什麼東西正從我房間的門外走過。

「是誰?」我喊道。

沒有應聲,這讓我開始感到害怕,接著,我聽到一個低沉的笑聲,是葛麗絲·普爾嗎?我一定要弄個清楚。於是我走下床,來到走廊,沒想到竟看到了在燃燒的蠟燭,緊接著是煙霧和燃燒的味道。

煙霧是從羅哲思德先生的臥室裡面飄出來的,因為他的房門是開著的,我走了進去,看到他的床幔竟然著火了!

P. 67

「快起來!快起來!」我大喊道,但是羅哲思德先生沒有動靜。

我衝去臉盆那邊,拿起水罐,往火焰沖水下去,然後再用花瓶的水潑向羅哲思德先生的臉,終於讓他醒了過來。

「是鬧水災嗎?」他喊道,發現自己躺在水灘中。

「不是啊,先生,失火啦!」我回答。

「發生什麼事了?」他邊起床邊問道。

我跟他說了事情的原委,他的神情顯得非常嚴肅。

接著,他說:「我去閣樓看一下,你待在這裡等我回來,不要有動作,也不要叫人來。」

當他再回來時,臉色蒼白,神情憂鬱。

「跟我想的一樣。」他說。

「怎麼回事，先生？」我問。

「你剛才說，你聽到了笑聲，這個聲音你以前有聽過嗎？」

P. 69

「有的，先生，是做女紅的葛麗絲‧普爾，那像是她的笑聲，她是個奇怪的人。」

「沒錯，是葛麗絲‧普爾——你說對了，就像你說的，她是個奇怪的人——很奇怪。簡，這件意外只有你和我知道，你懂我的意思嗎？請不要跟僕人們提這件事，我明天會跟他們說。現在，我們得去睡了。」

「是的，先生。那麼，晚安了，先生。」我說罷，準備轉身離開。

「簡，你要去哪裡？」羅哲思德先生喊道。

「先生，您說我可以走了。」

「那你好歹要好好道別一下，你剛剛才救了我的命！你起碼要和我握握手吧！」

他伸出他的手，我也向他伸手出去。他接住我的手，用雙手握住我的手。他

雙眼凝視著我，眼神中有一種奇怪的光火。

「我一看到你，就知道你是個特別的人。簡，你對我很好。」

「我很高興我剛才有醒過來。」我說完，便走回自己的房間，只是難以成眠。

第九章　白蘭絮‧英桂

P. 70

失眠的那一夜過後，我期盼再見到羅哲思德先生，但卻也感到害怕。不過，接下來的日子裡我沒再見到他了。我後來經過他的房間時，看到葛麗絲‧普爾正在縫他的新床幔。這事有點蹊蹺，我要試探她一下。

「葛麗絲‧普爾，早。怎麼會發生這麼奇怪的意外？真的沒有人被羅哲思德先生吵醒嗎？沒有人聽到他滅火的聲音嗎？」我說。

她抬眼看我，說道：「小姐，也許你聽到了聲音？」

「我是聽到了，我聽到了很奇怪的笑聲。」我壓低聲音說。

她又看了我一眼，說道：「那我想你每天晚上最好把你房間的門鎖好。」

這時，房間裡走進來了另一個僕人，她來跟我傳話，說斐法太太在等我，我只得離開葛麗絲‧普爾。

接下來幾天，這件神祕的事情一直盤旋在我心頭。羅哲思德先生怎麼不懲戒葛麗絲‧普爾所做的事情？我想去找羅哲思德先生，把話問清楚。我跟斐法太太打聽了他的去處。

「羅哲思德先生去了彌蔻特的另一頭找

朋友，那裡有一場盛宴。」

「他今天晚上會回來嗎？」我問。

P. 71

「哦，不會，我想他會在那裡待上一個星期，或是更久，他在宴會上很受歡迎，尤其是女士們。」

「哪一位女士？」我問。

「大部分的女士。」她回答：「不過他跟白蘭絮‧英桂特別的好。她是她們當中最美麗的女人了，她來參加過我們這裡辦的聖誕舞會，我見過她。」

「她長的什麼樣子？」

簡

- 簡為什麼對羅哲思德先生感到驚訝？
- 她為什麼要問起白蘭絮‧英桂的事？
- 你想簡對羅哲思德先生是怎樣的感情？

「她很修長，身材很好，有著迷人的橄欖色肌膚，一雙眸子像寶石一樣，還有一頭最烏黑亮麗的鬢髮！還有，她歌聲優美，我聽過他和羅哲思德先生一起高歌過。」

那天晚上，我一個人在房間時，我逼著自己去看鏡中的自己。

P. 73

「笨蛋！」我看著鏡中的自己，對自己說：「你是一個窮教師，而且長相平平，你怎麼會以為自己在羅哲思德先生的心中占有分量？看看白蘭絮‧英桂，再記住你自己是誰吧！」

兩個星期過去了，沒有羅哲思德先生的消息，我盡量抹去自己對他的感覺。我教導雅德蕾時很投入，空閒時間我就做針線活或是畫畫，我想把自己弄得很忙，我甚至考慮離開頌芙，換個工作。

後來，捎來了信件。斐法太太在讀信時，我心急的在一旁靜待。

「羅哲思德先生有提到什麼時候回來嗎？」我問道，盡量裝出不是太關切的樣子。

「有，他說三天後會和一群賓客回來，我們得準備他們的房間，等他們到來。」她回答。

有好多事得張羅，連我和雅德蕾都被找去幫忙打點。

一個午後，當我們正忙著時，我聽到兩個僕人談到了葛麗絲‧普爾。

「起碼她的薪水很好。」其中一個僕人說。

「哦，是啊，她的薪水是我們的五倍，不過她做那樣的工作，也是應得的啦。」

這時他們發現我在聽他們的對話，兩人於是快步走開。

現在，我確定頌芙有一樁不為人知的事情，但實情究竟如何，我仍然一無所知。

P. 75

薪水

- 你想葛麗絲‧普爾的薪水為什麼會那麼高？
- 你認為人們應該不同工就不同酬嗎？
- 在你的國家，什麼樣工作的薪水特別低或特別高？和夥伴討論。

賓客們蒞臨了，有人坐馬車來，有人騎馬來，我和雅德蕾站在樓梯間的窗口邊看著他們。有一個美麗的女子和羅哲思德先生並列騎馬而來，她的模樣就如斐法太太所描述的白蘭絮・英桂。

第二天晚上，我和雅德蕾被叫去參加他們的聚會。我坐在一旁的角落裡，看到雅德蕾很快就和所有的女士們交上了朋友。無疑的，白蘭絮・英桂是房間裡最美麗的女子，雖然她的姿態有些高傲。

用過咖啡之後，她和羅哲思德先生站在壁爐邊談話，我聽到她邀請羅哲思德先生高歌一曲，她要為他彈琴伴奏。我聆聽一下他們唱歌演奏，然後從側門離開。

羅哲思德先生來找我回去時，我人正在樓梯間。

「簡，你最近好嗎？」他問。

「我很好，先生。」

P. 76

「你怎麼不來客廳和我講講話？」

「先生，我怕打擾您，您好像很忙。」

「你的臉色看起來不是很好，好像不是很開心，怎麼了嗎？跟我說吧。」他說。

「沒事，先生，我沒事，我沒有不開心。」

「好吧，我今晚就放過你。不過，客人待在這裡的期間，我希望你每天晚上都能來參加我們的聚會，請務必參加。現在，晚了，我的……」

他打住，咬了一下嘴唇，然後轉身離開。

接下來這幾天，我看著羅哲思德先生和白蘭絮・英桂，雖然我愛羅哲思德先生，但是我並不會對白蘭絮小姐吃醋，她沒有可以讓人吃醋的地方。她是很漂亮，能彈一手好琴，歌喉也很好，但她內在空洞。她說的話，是從書上看來的，不是她個人的見地。她不溫柔，不善解人意，對雅德蕾沒有興趣。然而，很清楚的是，羅哲思德先生打算娶她，或許是基於家族或政治因素的考量，也許是因為她的社會地位和人脈對他很有幫忙。不過，我知道他並不愛她。

第十章　祕密

P. 77

當客人都還待在頌芙時，一天晚上，來了一個人，他表示有話要跟羅哲思德先生說。

「我叫梅西，剛從西印度群島過來。」他說。

他要我去通報羅哲思德先生，說有人來找他。我四處尋找羅哲思德先生，最後在圖書室看到了他。

「先生，他叫梅西，從西印度群島來的。我猜可能是牙買加的西班牙鎮吧。」

羅哲思德先生一聽到那個人的名字，臉色立刻轉白，他揪住我的手，彷彿停止呼吸。

「梅西！西印度群島！」他用奇怪的聲音說道。

「先生，您不舒服嗎？」我問。

「簡，我覺得很虛弱。」他一邊說，一邊差點跌倒。

「哦，先生，您可以靠著我。」

「簡，你的肩膀借我靠過一次，現在讓我再靠一下吧。」

「是的，先生，靠在這裡，抓著我的手。」

他坐下來，讓我坐在他身邊，他的兩隻手抓著我的雙手，用很憂心的眼神看著我。

「我的小朋友！我想和你一個人待在沙漠裡，那樣就什麼問題都不用面對了。」他說。

P.78

「先生，我能幫上什麼忙嗎？我可以為你做任何事。」

「簡，去把那個人帶過來，讓我和他單獨談。」

「是的，先生。」

我照辦了，許久之後，我在床上聽到了羅哲思德先生帶著梅西先生去客房。但願羅哲思德先生的麻煩已經結束了。

深夜裡，一個恐怖的尖叫聲驚醒了我，接著傳來男人的呼救聲。不一會兒，羅哲思德先生敲我的房門。

「簡，你起床穿衣服了嗎？」

「是的，先生。」

「那跟我走，盡量不要出聲。」

我跟著他走上閣樓，我原以為看到的人會是葛麗絲·普爾，想不到竟是梅西先生。他單獨一個人，坐在椅子上，一隻手臂上鮮血淋漓。

「幫他清理傷口，我去找醫生。」羅哲思德先生對我說：「在我離開這段時間，不可以跟他講話，一個字都不可講！還有，李察，你要是敢開口嚇這個女孩，你就會知道讓我整個抓狂起來會有多恐怖！」

他把門鎖上後便離開。我很害怕，但是我謹遵他的指示，不發一語地清理梅西先生的傷口。

「是什麼樣不為人知的事？一開始是失火，現在是有人流血。」我思索著。

當羅哲思德先生帶著醫生回來時，我很高興。醫生將傷口包紮上繃帶，然後和羅哲思德先生一起將梅西先生扶下樓。他們讓他上一輛馬車，就在僕人醒來之前，送他離開了。

P.79

天邊逐漸泛白，春天的空氣很清新。這時，羅哲思德先生突然從樹叢中摘下一朵玫瑰花，交到我手上。

「簡，要再謝謝你了。」他一邊說，一邊牽起我的手，緊緊地握住。

那天下午，我收到了佳慈賀府邸寄來的信。約翰·瑞德過世了，舅媽瑞德夫人也不久於人世，她想見我最後一面。

於是我立刻去找羅哲思德先生，請他允許我離開。我看到他時，他正和英桂小姐在打撞球。

他看到我來，便隨我走出房間。

「簡，怎麼了？」他問。

「先生，請允許我離開一、兩個星期。」

「你要做什麼？要去哪裡？」

我跟他說了舅媽的事，羅哲思德先生不明白我何苦回去，不過他最後還是支付了我一些薪水，並且要我承諾一定會再回來。

「先生，我還有些話想說。我知道你打算把英桂小姐娶進門，等你結婚了，雅德蕾也就要去上學了，到時候這裡就不需要我，所以我會另覓工作。」我說。

P.80

我不想待在頌芙，看著白蘭絮·英桂

成為羅哲思德夫人。

「簡，你先別這樣做。」他說。

他又再度要我承諾一定會盡快回來，最後才放我走。

我抵達佳慈賀府邸時，來迎接我的是蓓詩，她先讓我用了茶。屋子裡的每一樣陳設都一如往昔，我在這裡生活過的回憶，開始一幕幕湧上來。

稍後，蓓詩帶我去臥室見瑞德夫人。我決定把對這個女人的所有痛恨情緒都拋掉，我只想原諒她對我所做的一切。

我走向她，她還是一張嚴厲冷酷的臉。我撫摸她、親吻她，她都沒有回應，於是我明白她對我的感受還是跟我小時候一樣。在她心裡，我是個壞女孩，她並不想改變她對我的成見。我感到受傷，惱羞成怒，不過我決定不要因她而心煩。

舅媽想跟我說些什麼，不過她一直等到確定旁邊都沒人了才啟口。

她說：「簡‧愛，我對你做了兩件壞事情，我現在很後悔，我想在死之前跟你說清楚。第一件事情，我答應丈夫要視如己出地把你撫養長大，我食言了。另一件事情，你去我的珠寶盒那邊，把珠寶盒打開，裡面有一封信，你把信拿出來。」

P. 81

我照她所說的去做，把信拿了過來。

「你把信唸出來。」她說。

夫人：

你可以把我的姪女簡‧愛的住址給我嗎？跟我說說她過得怎麼樣吧。

我想寫信給她，請她過來馬德拉跟我一起住。我有一份不錯的工作，但我沒有結婚，也沒有孩子，我想領養她，等我百年之後，就把所有的東西都留給她。

約翰‧愛，於馬德拉

信上署名的時間是三年前的某一天。

「你為什麼沒跟我提這件事？」我問。

「因為我太討厭你了，怎樣都不想幫你這個忙。你小時候是怎樣對我說話的，這我忘不了。」

P. 82

瑞德夫人

· 簡‧愛小時候是怎樣對瑞德夫人說話的？如果你不記得了，可以翻回第 24 頁查一下。

· 你記得有人對你做過什麼不好的事嗎？你可以原諒、忘記嗎？和夥伴討論。

「舅媽，對不起，我那時候還小。」我說。

她對我的道歉不感興趣，繼續說道：「我報復了你。我寫信跟你叔叔說你死了。好啦，我說完了，你想怎樣就怎樣吧，你天生就是我的剋星。」

「舅媽，別再這麼想了。親親我，我們把過去忘了吧。」我回答。

我把嘴唇靠近她的臉頰，但她把臉別過去。她至今還是無法愛我。

「你是愛我還是恨我，都任隨你。」我最後說道：「我已經徹底原諒你了，去請求上帝的寬恕吧，安息了。」

那天夜裡，瑞德夫人撒手了。

我原本計畫在佳慈賀府邸只停留一、兩個星期，不過等我啟程返回頌芙時，已經過了一個月。

第十一章 返回頌芙

P. 83

我不希望斐法太太派馬車來接我，所以決定從彌蔻特步行回頌芙府邸。我開始動身，今晚這個夏夜並不是太晴朗，不過田地裡可見許多農民在幹活。

我心情愉快，但我並不清楚原因何在，我又不是要回自己的家，那裡也沒有真正的友人。「但是斐法太太和雅德蕾看到我會很開心。不過，你很清楚你心裡想的是另一個人，而那個人卻不想你。」我對自己說。

我急著想趕快回到府邸，便抄捷徑穿過田地。突然間，他就在那裡！羅哲思德先生坐在牆堵上，他手裡拿著一本書和一枝筆。

「簡‧愛，你去哪裡了？你把我忘了嗎？」他說。

「先生，我當然沒有忘了你。」我回答。為什麼我的身子在顫抖？為什麼我的話這麼難以說出口？

「快回家吧，好好讓疲憊的腳歇歇！」他一邊說，一邊下牆堵，讓路給我過去。

我想沉著地走開，但某種力量讓我停下腳步，我轉過身說道：「羅哲思德先生，謝謝您！能再回到你的身邊，我出奇的開心，有你在的地方，就是我的家，我唯一的家。」

P. 85

接著我走得這麼快，羅哲思德先生要追上來也不可能。頌芙府邸的每個人看到我都很高興，我覺得我是被愛的。用過茶點後，我和斐法太太、雅德蕾一起坐在斐法太太的房間裡，很開心大家又能擁有彼此的相伴。

那個夏天，氣候很好，天天陽光普照。一天晚上，將雅德蕾送上床之後，我來到外面的花園，享受沁涼的空氣。不久，我就發現夜間出來散步的人，不只有我一個。

「夏天的頌芙，真是一個好地方，對吧，簡？」羅哲思德先生說。

「是的，先生。」

「你現在一定很喜歡府邸了，只可惜你得另找工作了。」

「先生，我一定要另找工作？一定要離開頌芙嗎？」我問。

「我想是的，簡，我下個月就要結婚了。我替你在愛爾蘭找到了一份新的工作。」

這個消息如同晴天霹靂，我想保持平靜，未料淚水從我臉上開始悄悄地滑落。

「愛爾蘭遠在天邊呀，先生。」我說。

P. 86

「的確，簡，我很遺憾要把你送走。我有時候對你有一種奇怪的感覺，尤其是當你離我像現在這麼近的時候，我覺得有一條線緊緊繫著你我的心，我感到如果和你分離，線就會斷掉，我會受傷。不過，你不會有這種感覺，我想你會忘掉我的。」

「先生，我不會忘記你的，不過如果我

得走，我就走。我愛頌芙這個地方，我無法再那麼快樂了，一想到以後永遠不會再看到你，我就悲傷萬分。不過，如果我一定要離開……」

「你為什麼一定要離開？」

「先生，因為您的新娘子。」

「我的新娘子？什麼新娘子？我沒有新娘子！」

「你之後就會有了。」

「沒錯，是會有。」

「所以我一定要走，你自己是這樣跟我說的。」

「不！你一定要留下來。」他一邊說，一邊抱住了我。我想掙開他的懷抱，他卻把我摟得更緊。

「簡，請不要再把我推開了，你像隻發狂想逃脫的野鳥。」

「我不是鳥，沒有籠子也沒有網圍住我，我是一個自由的人，可以對自己的人生做出決定。現在，放開我吧。」

我掙開，站立在他的面前。

「那你就決定你自己的命運，我給你我的手、我的心，分享我所擁有的一切。簡，嫁給我吧！」他說。

我不知道要如何回應他，我想他是在嘲弄我。

「我能相信您嗎？您真的愛我嗎？您真心希望我成為您的妻子嗎？」我最後終於說道。

P. 87

「我是真心的！真的！」

「那麼，先生，我會嫁給您。」

「是『愛德華』，不是『先生』，我的小小妻子！」

那一個早上，我一直在想羅哲思德先生的求婚是否只是一場夢。為了確認那不是夢，我要再聽一次同樣的話，於是用過早餐後，我去找了他。

「我的小簡‧愛，很快就要變成簡‧羅哲思德了！」他一邊說，一邊親吻我。

這一刻，我湧上了一股更甚於喜悅的強烈感覺，那幾近於一種恐懼感。

他提到了婚禮，也說到要買什麼樣的衣服給我，要帶我去什麼地方玩，要送給我什麼樣的珠寶。

我告訴他：「我並不想要珠寶，不過我有兩件事想要問您。第一件事，你為什麼要裝出想娶白蘭絮‧英桂的樣子？」

P. 88

「因為我希望你能愛我，就像我那麼愛你一樣，所以故意讓你吃醋。那第二件事呢？」他回答。

「請跟斐法太太講我們的婚事，她人很好，我很喜歡她，我不想讓她對我有不好的感覺。」

羅哲思德先生答應了我的請求，我便走回我的房間。稍後，我下樓去找斐法太太。

她平靜地看著我，說道：「我真不敢相信，你真的要嫁給羅哲思德先生嗎？他愛你嗎？」她問。

我感覺很受傷，眼裡湧上了淚水。

「我很抱歉讓你難過了，但是我一定要勸你小心為妙，事情往往不是表面上看起來的那樣。」斐法太太說。

一個月過去了，離我大喜的日子愈來愈近。我的箱子收拾停當，禮服和面紗就掛在衣櫥裡。

之後的一個晚上，羅哲思德先生出門辦事不在家。我做了一個惡夢，驚醒過

來,卻看到我的房間裡點著一根蠟燭。我環顧了一下,竟在衣櫥那邊看到了一個高高的女性身影,她正打量著我的禮服。她拉出面紗披上,在鏡前看著自己。接著,她把面紗拉下,撕成兩半。我透過鏡影看到了她的臉龐,她看起來黑黑的,樣子很野蠻。我想我嚇得昏了過去。

P.90

婚禮前夕,我跟羅哲思德先生提起這個女人的事。那是葛麗絲·普爾,他說。我想採信他的話,卻騙不了自己。

「簡,我看得出來你緊張了。你今晚和雅德蕾一起睡吧,要把房門鎖好。」他說。

我照做了。我抱著小女孩,感覺安全多了,只不過我還是睡不著。

隔天一大清早,蘇菲幫我穿上結婚禮服。在下樓之前,我站在鏡前,認不出鏡中的自己。

羅哲思德先生前往教堂時很心急,要我加緊腳步跟著,等我們抵達教堂門口時,我已經氣喘吁吁。

教堂裡很安靜,只有教區牧師和執事,以及站在角落裡看著羅哲思德族墓的兩個人影。之後,婚禮開始,教區牧師宣讀了我們結婚的意願,並問我們是否存有不應結婚的理由。

這時,教堂後方傳來了一個聲音,說道:「不應該有這場婚禮。」

「快繼續!」羅哲思德先生生氣地吼道。

「我們把問題弄清楚了,我才能繼續。先生,請告訴我們,為什麼不應該有這場婚禮?」教區牧師說。

講那句話的人趨前過來,他表明自己是一位從倫敦來的律師,名叫簿格思先生。

「因為羅哲思德先生已婚,而且妻子尚在人世。」他說。

P.91

我看著羅哲思德先生,他的臉色一陣慘白。

「你有證明嗎?」羅哲思德先生問道。

簿格思先生從口袋裡取出一份文件,對著我們讀了起來。

「我可以證實,十月二十日(那是十五年前的日子),愛德華·羅哲思德先生在牙買加的西班牙鎮,迎娶了我的姊姊貝兒妲·安東尼達·梅西。我這裡有一份結婚證明的副件。簽署人李察·梅西。」

他又說有一個證人可以證明這位女士尚在人世。

這時簿格思的身後出現了一張蒼白的臉,那是梅西先生。

「你能告訴我們,羅哲思德夫人是否還在人世嗎?」

「她還在人世,而且就在頌芙府邸。」

梅西緩緩地說道：「我四月時才在那裡見過她，我是她的弟弟。」

「她人就在頌芙府邸？不可能！先生，我在這裡住了這麼多年，沒聽過頌芙府邸有一位羅哲思德夫人！」教區牧師驚呼道。

「那是因為我小心不讓別人知道這件事情。」羅哲思德先生說：「你們大家都跟我走吧，我們去頌芙府邸，我讓你們看看我的『妻子』。」

P. 92

羅哲思德先生牽起我的手，我們匆匆返回頌芙。當我抵達府邸時，我再度喘不過來，不過這回是出於震驚。教區牧師、執事、簿格思先生、梅西先生，他們跟在我們的後面。

那位『妻子』

- 你有想過羅哲思德先生的妻子是誰嗎？
- 你想，在這種時刻，簡・愛的內心會作何感受？

我們大家走上樓，一起來到閣樓。葛麗絲・普爾當時坐在爐火邊，不過她不是單獨一人。在房間的另一頭，有一個跑來跑去的身影，就像動物一樣，而且像狗那樣咆哮著。一看到羅哲思德先生，牠站了起來，把遮住臉的蓬髮撩開，我立刻認出了那張臉，那是撕破我的面紗的那位女子！

突然，她撲向羅哲思德先生，想要咬他。她很強壯，羅哲思德先生想辦法抓住她的手，葛麗絲・普爾一起幫忙將她綁在一張椅子上。

「這就是我的妻子！看看她，再看看我想要娶的那位無邪的年輕女孩！你們能指責我去追求一點點的幸福嗎？你們現在走吧！我要確保我真正的妻子安全地被鎖在這裡。」

第十二章　逃離

P. 94

我回到房間，脫下結婚禮服，坐了下來，我感到疲憊又虛弱。我開始思索　，昨天，我是簡・愛，就要當新娘子了，充滿著愛和希望。而今天，我一無所有。

我一樣愛著羅哲思德先生，但是我知道我無法再和他在一起了。

傍晚時分，我終於下了床，打開房門。羅哲思德先生這時就坐在房門外的一張椅子上，他在等著我。

「你終於出來了。簡，你能原諒我嗎？」他說。

我立即原諒了他，但是我沒有說出口。

「簡，把你的手給我吧，我想把一切解釋清楚，聽我講幾分鐘的話，求求你！」

他跟我說，他的父親逼他娶貝兒妲，因為她家境殷實，而他自己的家庭當時需要金錢。他預先並不曉得她神經錯亂，事後知道已經來不及了。

「我們可以離開，離開頌芙，開始新的生活。」他繼續說道。

「不，我要離開你和頌芙。我對你的愛更深了，只是，我不能留下來，我要開始另一個新的人生。你的妻子還在世，我不能當你的情婦。」

羅哲思德先生懇求我跟他在一起，我

想説「好」，但卻不行。

我打包了我少許的東西，離開了頌芙。

P. 95

我知道我一定要離開這裡，離開那個我愛的男人，離得愈遠愈好。兩天過去了，我在惠夸司這個地方下了馬車。

現在，我沒有盤纏，形單影隻。我開始步行，走了一段很長的時間，儘管我又累又餓。之後，開始下起大雨，我環顧四周找地方躲雨，最後看到了一間小木屋。透過窗戶，我看到裡面有兩個女孩和一位老婦人。我敲了門，請求幫助，但老婦人打發我走。我實在累垮了，就在門口外倒了下來。我所有的希望、氣力，都蕩然無存了。

「我就要死了！」我大聲地對自己説。

「凡夫終須一死。」黑暗中傳來説話聲。

「是誰在那裡？」我驚嚇地問。

出現了一個男人，他大聲地朝門敲去。

「辛晉先生，是您嗎？」屋裡的老婦人問。

「是，是我。漢娜，快把門打開。」接著他對我説：「年輕女孩，站起來吧，進屋子裡來。」

我努力撐著地照做了。不一會兒，我就坐在一間乾淨、燈火明亮的廚房裡，眼前是一杯熱牛奶和幾塊麵包。一個女孩問了我的名字。

「簡・葉里特。」我回答。

「你是迷路了嗎？我們可以聯絡一下你的家人或朋友嗎？」男人問道。

P. 97

「這世界上只有我一個人。」我如是回答。

之後，他們帶我上樓，讓我睡在一張溫暖乾爽的床上。

我一連睡了三天。我發了高燒，身子動不了。

到了第五天，我才有力氣可以起床。我靜靜地緩步走下樓，來到廚房裡，見了這些照顧我的好心人。那位年紀較長的女僕漢娜正在烤麵包，她給了我一個微笑，要我在爐火邊坐下來，然後開始問起我的事。

「你這樣乞討很久了嗎？」她問。

我聽了很意外，我跟她説我不是乞丐。

「那你怎麼沒有家，也沒有錢？」她問。

「我會盡快找到工作和住處。」我回答。

之後，她跟我説起那兩位女孩，黛安娜・黎華斯和瑪麗・黎華斯是姊妹，辛晉先生是她們的哥哥，他在鄰村擔任教區牧師。

這時，他們都走了進來。他們親切地問候我，我對他們的殷勤招待表達感謝之情。他們也有很多問題要問我，我簡略地跟他們説明了一下我的情況。

「我未婚，沒有家庭。」我開始説道：「我之前待在蘿霧學校，在那裡擔任教師。後來我找到了家庭教師的工作，不過就在幾天前，非得離開那裡不可了。離開的原因，恕難相告，不過決非是因為做錯了什麼事，我不是罪犯。現在，我又要重新找工作，掙錢糊口了。」

P. 98

「所以説，你是一位老師囉？」辛晉説：「下個月，這裡有一間新的女子教會學校就要開辦了，我們目前還沒有找到老師。老師的年薪是三十英鎊，會提供女老師一間住宿的木屋，你有興趣當這間學校的老師嗎？」

「謝謝您，黎華斯先生，有的，我非常有興趣。」我回答。

我和黎華斯一家人度過了愉快的幾個星期之後，大夥兒開始各自的生活——我搬進了我的木屋，黛安娜和瑪麗返回她們的工作，擔任家庭教師，辛晉先生繼續他教區牧師的工作崗位。

P. 99

我學校裡的學生都是純樸的鄉下女孩、農家女兒，我教她們閱讀、編織、縫補和歌唱。我工作賣力，很忙碌，但我樂在其中。只有在夜深人靜的時刻，過去的生活才會浮現心頭，我也常常會去想像和羅哲思德先生重逢的光景。

辛晉先生每天都會來學校，教導一個小時的宗教課程。放假時，他也會來看我。有一次他來訪時，特別請求要看我的畫作。

我很樂意和他分享。他一邊翻著畫紙，一邊誇獎我畫得很好。這時，他突然打住，望著那張空白的紙，那是我作畫時用來墊手用的紙。我不知道他是看到了什麼，他只是很快地站起身來，告辭離開。

第十三章 新生活

P. 100

第二天，辛晉先生又來了。

「我有一點事想跟你談，請過來跟我一起坐在爐火前。」

待我們兩人坐定後，他從口袋裡掏出一封信，拿在手上。

「幾個星期前，我收到了簿格思先生從倫敦寄來的這封信，裡面細說了一個叫簡·愛的女孩的事情。昨天，在你的畫作中，我看到一張紙上面寫著這個名字，你的名字並不是簡·葉里特，對吧？你叫簡·愛。」他說。

「黎華斯先生，信裡頭有提到羅哲思德先生嗎？」這是我僅僅只想到要說的事。

「沒有，簿格思先生要我幫忙找簡·愛，因為他有重要的事要跟她說。他登報尋人，斐法太太看到了，便寫信給他。她跟他說了細節，簿格思先生要跟你說的是，你在馬德拉的叔叔過世了，他把所有的遺產都留給你，現在你是一位很有身價的女人了。」

「我很有身價？」

「是的，你身價兩萬英鎊。」

我吃驚地看著他。

「可是，請跟我說，簿格思先生為什麼要寫信跟你說我的事？」我聽到自己在問道。

P. 101

「我媽媽姓愛，她有兩個兄弟，一個娶了佳慈賀的簡·瑞德小姐，另一個叫約翰·愛，他去了馬德拉。簿格思先生是愛先生的律師，他找不到你，便聯絡了我們。」

「這麼說，你媽媽是我爸爸的妹妹？」

「是的。」

「所以也就是我的姑姑？」

他點點頭。

「那麼，你、黛安娜、瑪麗，就是我的表兄弟姊妹了？」

「是的！」

我興奮得拍起手來，我有和我相親相愛的家人了！我不再是孑然一身了！

「我太開心、太開心了！」

「你聽到有家人，比聽到有遺產還開心。」

「當然啦，我以前孤伶伶一個人，而現在，我有家人了！明天就寫信給黛安娜和瑪麗，要她們回來。我有這筆錢了，她們以後不用再工作了。」

家人

- 和朋友把簡的家族族譜畫出來吧。
- 你覺得擁有家人是很重要的嗎？為什麼？

P.102

我決定這兩萬英鎊要由我們四個人共享。我辭去學校的教學工作，搬回到木屋和表姊妹黛安娜、瑪麗一起住，辛晉仍住在教區公館，但他常常回來看我們。這是我一段幸福的時光。

有一天，辛晉跟我們說，他要前往印度擔任傳教士。他開始學印度斯坦語，並且要我陪他。我答應了，之後我們花了許多小時一起學印度話。我愈來愈了解他，我發現他是一個非常嚴肅的人，別人很難取悅他。

我還是很想念羅哲思德先生，我知道我不能去找他，但是我想知道他過得好不好，於是我決定寫信給斐法太太。

兩個月過去了，音信杳無，我又再寫了一封信。日子一天天過去，郵差未曾為我捎來什麼，我感到心煩意亂。

夏天到來了，一個陽光閃爍的上午，辛晉找我去散步。我們坐在一塊岩石上歇息時，他向我求婚，並請我跟他一起去印度。

我直接拒絕了他，而且可能拒絕得太快了。我不愛辛晉，我也不認為他是真正愛我，他是想找我去幫忙他做傳教的工作。

我知道我的心依然歸屬於羅哲思德先生。我多麼想得知他的消息，於是我決定去一趟頌芙，親自去看看他過得如何。

P.104

我跟表姊妹說我要離開幾天，她們沒有多問我要上哪兒去。

我一路上大多都搭乘馬車，一直到最後兩英里時，才用步行的方式前往頌芙。我快步走著，有時甚至是用跑的。再度看到這片林子，我很開心，不過最主要的是我等不及想再看見羅哲思德先生的臉。

終於，我來到了圍著花園的那道牆。我拐進轉角，渴望看到宅第，我期待再見到頌芙府邸的光彩，然而，映入眼廉的卻是斷垣殘壁。

房子的正面依舊矗立在那裡，但是卻沒有了屋頂，也沒有煙囪，沒有窗戶。這裡一片死寂，剎那間我明白了為什麼我的信會石沉大海。

災難是怎麼發生的？有人罹難嗎？

四下無人，沒有人可以回答這些問題，也沒有蛛絲馬跡可以說明這場災難是怎麼一回事。

災難

- 你能回答簡的問題嗎？
- 你想頌芙府邸發生了什麼事？

P. 105

最後，是當地一家旅舍老闆跟我説了始末。

他説：「那是去年秋天的事，在家庭女教師不見了之後（這事説來又話頭長了），羅哲思德先生送走了管家和雅德蕾小姐，把自己關在宅院裡。後來，有一個晚上，房子就失火了，聽説肇事者是住在閣樓裡的一位瘋女人，人們後來發現她是羅哲思德先生的夫人，她想燒自己的房間，還有樓下的一個房間。還好的是，僕人們都及時逃了出來，但那個瘋女人往屋頂上走，羅哲思德先生企圖救她，可是她卻往下一跳，摔死了。」

「還有任何其他人罹難嗎？」我問。

「沒有，不過，可憐的羅哲思德先生……」他回答。

「他怎麼了？」我問，害怕聽到他會怎麼回答。

「羅哲思德先生吃了很多苦，一塊燃燒的木頭掉下來砸中了他，他傷的很重。他的命是救回來了，可是現在失明了。」

「他人在哪裡？他現在住在哪裡？」

「他住在他一座農場的屋子裡，離這裡三十英里遠，老約翰夫婦在照顧他。」

「你可以帶我去嗎？我會付你一筆錢。」

「我很樂意，女士。路上我再跟你説家庭女教師的事吧。」

「這倒不用了，那些事我已經知道了。」我回答。

在接近屋子一英里遠時，我付錢給旅館老闆，請他返回。我想徒步走過去。

P. 106

夜幕將垂，傳入耳裡的只有雨滴打在樹葉上的聲音。

「這裡會有人嗎？」我走向房子，自問道。

是的，有人。我聽到走動的聲音，餘暉中走出一個身影，佇足在階梯上。那是一個男人，他沒有戴帽子。他伸出手，感受雨水。那是我的主人，愛德華·羅哲思德！

失明

- 想像一下，失明的話會是怎樣的情況。先和一個夥伴討論，然後全班同學再一起討論。
- 視障者在日常生活中會遇到什麼樣的困難？一一列出來。

我停下腳步，看著他。我想好好地看看他，當然，他是看不到我的，他已經失明了。

在身體外觀上，他看起來和一年前沒有兩樣，他還是很強健，背部直挺挺的，一頭黑髮如昔，但我在他的臉上看到了絕望。他捉摸地移動了幾步，伸出兩手去感覺前方的路，然後他放棄了，轉身進到屋子裡。

P. 108

我靜待了一會兒，然後才敲門。來開門的，是頌芙府邸以前的一位年長女僕瑪麗。她不敢相信眼前的人是我，我牽著她的手，跟隨她走進廚房。我們坐在爐火前，我跟她講了我所有的事。這

時，傳來了一個鈴聲，那是羅哲思德先生，他想要喝水。

「托盤給我，我送過去給他。」我說。

我踏進房間時，身體顫抖，心跳急促。

羅哲思德先生聽到房門打開的聲音，他轉過身來。因為看不到，他又把身子轉回去，嘆了一口氣。

我拿著水杯走向他。

「瑪麗，是你吧？」

「瑪麗在廚房。」我說。

「你是誰？是誰？」他問道。「回答我！你再說一次！」他命令道。

「我今天晚上才剛剛到達這裡。」我說。

「這個聲音！是她的聲音！我是瘋了嗎？過來，讓我摸摸看你！」

我把手交到他的手上。

「這是她的手指！」他喊道。接著，他摸我的肩膀、我的脖子、我的腰。「沒有錯！這是她的身材大小，簡！」

「親愛的主人，我找到你了，我回到你身邊了，我再也不要離開你了！」我回答。

我用雙臂環抱住他，親吻他可憐的雙眼。

然後，我跟他說了我的新家人、我的

財產，也說了我為什麼要回到頌芙，還有我聽說了失火的事。

第十四章　尾聲

P.110

讀者，我們結婚了。我們有一場安靜而美好的婚禮。

我寫信跟表兄弟姊妹說了這件事，黛安娜和瑪麗為我們感到高興，但是辛晉沒有回信給我。

我去學校看了雅德蕾，她再見到我時好開心。她看起來蒼白瘦弱，我發現她學校裡的老師很嚴格，便決定把她帶走，讓她上另一間離我們比較近的學校。那裡的新老師和善多了，她現在的功課表現也很好，我們常常去找她。

轉眼間，我已經結婚十年了，我們為彼此而活著。我們可以走上一整天，從不曾厭倦彼此的相伴。我們是天造地設的一對，我們過著琴瑟和鳴的生活。

在結婚最初兩年，我是愛德華的眼睛，他透過我的眼睛來看一切事物。後來，有一天，他跟我說他可以看到一點點東西了。我們遵照倫敦一位醫師的指示，最後，他的一隻眼睛恢復了視力，雖然不是看得很清楚，但足以應付行走。當我把我們的第一個寶寶放進他的臂彎裡時，他看到孩子的眼睛長得跟他一樣，在失火之前，他的眼睛又大又亮又黑。

我的愛德華和我，我們過著幸福的日子。而我們所愛的人的幸福，也讓我們更加、更加的幸福了。

ANSWER KEY

Before Reading

P. 8
1 1. c   2. d   3. a   4. b

P. 9
3 a. Family   b. School   c. House
4 a. House   b. School   c. Family

P. 10
5 a. benches   b. piano   c. easel
d. slates   e. sewing   f. advertisement
g. drawing   h. stool

P. 11
6 a. easel   b. advertisement   c. stool
d. slates   e. drawing   f. sewing
g. benches   h. piano

P. 12
7 1. coach   2. on a horse   3. on foot
4. open carriage

P. 18
• orphan, no money, not happy, not welcome

P. 28
• She is in shock. Everything seems big, long and very mechanical.

P. 31
• He is strict. A tall stern man. He thinks Jane Eyre is wicked after what Mrs Reed told him.

P. 37
• Because she is not deceitful or a liar.

P. 46
• She is ready for a new experience.
• She is bored.

P. 49
• He is a little mysterious. He is very rich.

P. 58
• Mr Rochester.

P. 82
• She answered her back. She told Mrs Reed what she thought of her and said she didn't love her.

P. 92
• The mad lady in the attic.

After Reading

P. 113
3 a. F   b. T   c. T   d. F   e. F   f. F
g. T   h. F   i. T   j. F   k. T   l. F

P. 114
4
a. She hated it and couldn't wait to leave.
d. After the typhus there were improvements with the introduction of a committee and better conditions for the girls.
e. She met Mrs Fairfax, who was the housekeeper. She met Mr Rochester much later.
f. She liked him straight away but didn't think he was handsome.
h. She knew there was a mystery but

didn't know what it was until the day of her wedding.

j. He was very impatient and nervous.

l. She heard this from the innkeeper.

5 a. 2   b. 4   c. 1   d. 3

6

a. Mr Brocklehurst makes her stand on this and then humiliates her in front of the whole class.

b. St John Rivers sees Jane Eyre's real name and then realizes who she is. She then becomes an heiress and discovers she has family.

c. The advertisement helps Jane to get the job at Thornfield Hall.

P. 115

7 plain, honest, sincere, daring, courageous, strong

8 a. 3   b. 2   c. 9   d. 4   e. 1   f. 11   g. 7   h. 10   i. 5   j. 12   k. 6   l. 8

P. 116

9 a. character   b. hero   c. women   d. fire   e. love   f. element

P. 117

10

a. Gateshead Hall: Bessie, John Reed, Aunt Reed

b. Lowood Institution: Mr Brocklehurst, Miss Temple, Helen Burns

c. Thornfield Hall: Grace Poole, Bertha, Mr Mason, Mrs Fairfax, Adela, Blanche Ingram, Mr Rochester

d. Cottage near Whitcross: St John Rivers, Diana Rivers, Mary Rivers

P. 118

11 a. 2   b. 5   c. 4   d. 3   e. 1

12 a. 2   b. 3   c. 4   d. 1

P. 119

13 14

• Helen Burns forgives the cruel teacher and tries to be a better person. She forgives and forgets.

• Mr Rochester forgives Celine and takes in her daughter Adela as his ward and helps her even if she goes off with another man.

• Jane Eyre forgives Mrs Reed for everything she does.

14 Mrs. Reed; John, Eliza, Georgiana; Jane, St. John, Diana, Mary

P. 120

15 a. made   b. let   c. made   d. made   e. made   f. made   g. let

16

• She managed to get out of her room to set fire to Mr Rochester's room. She managed to hurt her brother when he came to see her. She managed to get out of her room and frighten Jane before her wedding with her veil. She managed to make her presence felt with her laugh.

P. 121

17

a. How long did Jane Eyre live at Gateshead Hall. She lived there for the first ten years of her life.

b. How long did Jane Eyre stay at Lowood? She stayed at Lowood for eight years – six as a pupil and two as a teacher.

c. How long did Jane Eyre have to stand on stool? She had to stand on the stool for half an hour.

d. How long did Jane Eyre stay at Gateshead at the time of Aunt Reed's death? She stayed there for a month.

e. How long was Jane Eyre engaged to Mr Rochester? She was engaged to him for one month.

18

a. John Reed is wicked and cruel because he bullies and hurts Jane.

b. Helen Burns is humble and obedient because she accepts criticism and tries not to make mistakes.

c. Jane Eyre is sincere and honest because she always says what she thinks.

d. Mr Rochester is strange and complicated because he changes mood often and is not predictable. He is hiding something that makes him very sad.

TEST

P. 122

1 a. 2   b. 1   c. 2   d. 2

P. 123

2 a. T   b. F   c. F   d. F   e. T   f. T
g. T   h. F

3

b. He makes her stand on a stool in the middle of the classroom.

c. She does the sewing and looks after Bertha.

d. He is pale and weak when he hears he has arrived.

h. She meets him at another house because Thornfield Hall has been burnt down.

國家圖書館出版品預行編目資料

簡愛 / Charlotte Brontë 著；安卡斯 譯.
—初版. —[臺北市] : 寂天文化, 2015.1 面；
公分. 中英對照

ISBN 978-986-318-325-9 (25K平裝附光碟片)

1. 英語　2. 讀本

805.18   103027705

原著 _ Charlotte Brontë
改寫 _ Frances Mariani
譯者 _ 安卡斯
校對 _ 陳慧莉
製程管理 _ 宋建文
出版者 _ 寂天文化事業股份有限公司
電話 _ +886-2-2365-9739
傳真 _ +886-2-2365-9835
網址 _ www.icosmos.com.tw
讀者服務 _ onlineservice@icosmos.com.tw
出版日期 _ 2015年1月 初版一刷（250101）

郵撥帳號 _ 1998620-0 寂天文化事業股份有限公司